LIGATURE & LATTE

CONNIE CAFE MYSTERIES
BOOK 2

MAISY MARPLE

BECOME A VIP READER!

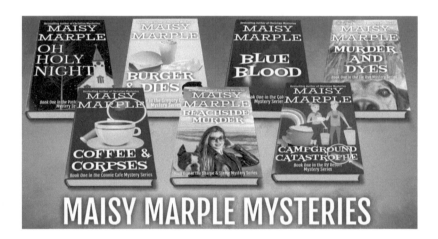

To get updates on current projects and gain access to special contests and prizes, click on the image and sign up!

ALSO BY MAISY MARPLE

*Visit Maisy Marple's Author Page on Amazon to read
any of the titles below!*

Connie Cafe Series

Coffee & Corpses

Ligature & Latte

Autumn & Autopsies

Pumpkins & Poison

Death & Decaf

Turkey & Treachery

Mistletoe & Memories

Snow & Sneakery

Repairs & Renovations

Bagels & Bible Study

S'more Jesus

Proverbs & Preparations

Sharpe & Steele Series

Beachside Murder

Sand Dune Slaying

Boardwalk Body Parts

RV Resort Mystery Series

Campground Catastrophe

Bad News Barbecues

Sunsets and Bad Bets

Short Stories

Forty Years Together

Long Story Short

The Best Gift of All

Miracle at the Mall

The Ornament

The Christmas Cabin

Cold Milk at Midnight

Short Story Collections

Hot Cocoa Christmas

Unapologetically Christian Essays

Reason for the Season

God is Not Santa Claus

Free Will is Messy

Fear Not

Not About this World

We Are All Broken

Veritas

God Ain't Your Butler

An Argument for Hate

Agape Love (With Pastor Michael Golden)

Addiction Help

Hard Truths: Overcoming Alcoholism One Second At A Time

1

This was the day my dreams came true!

I, Connie Cafe, was going to meet with James Popper, the best realtor in Coffee Creek.

The journey that started when I was a child, dreaming of imaginary dragons in my backyard while my father drank piping hot cups of black coffee, was about to become my reality. I was going to open my very own coffee shop in Coffee Creek.

Everything got sidetracked for me after my father died. I'd moved home to live with my mother and started working for some big chain coffee shop and getting the scoop on local stories for the *Coffee Creek Gazette.*

Long story short, a few months back, I was reporting on the Coffee Creek Golf Tournament and found David Gardner, the best golfer in Coffee Creek, dead in a water hazard. Well, timing is everything, apparently, because I was the main suspect in the case — that was until I proved my innocence.

Thankfully, that mess went away, and my mother, Roberta Cafe, encouraged me to open up my dream coffee shop in Coffee Creek. And my best friend, Reba, said she was going to come work for me.

The time was here for me to open up *Connie's Cafe* on Main Street, right in the heart of Coffee Creek!

But before I got ahead of myself, I had to find a building. That was where James came in.

"It's good to see you looking excited about something," my mother said, handing me a big mug of java as I walked into the kitchen of our old farmhouse. "It's been a while."

I nodded, accepting the dark roast with open arms. "I agree. I feel like I've been in a ten-year funk."

"Twelve," my mother winked. "But who's counting?"

"Apparently, not me."

"So, how many places are you looking at today?"

"I think James said he had three. Two of them are on Main Street, and the other one's a little off the beaten path." I rolled my eyes. "I told him that I didn't want to be anywhere other than Main Street, but he insisted. I guess you can get away with being pushy when you've got the reputation he has."

"I guess," my mother shrugged. "Just promise me one thing, honey?"

"What's that?"

"Promise me that you will make the choice that's best for you. This is your dream. Don't let someone else try to tell you how to live your life."

"As she tries to tell me how to live my life," I snorted. Coffee went flying onto the counter and farmhouse floor. I was so excited I couldn't even get the joke out without just about choking on my coffee.

"Serves you right." My mother handed me a paper towel to clean up the mess I'd made. "I'm not trying to run your life, ya know. I just want you to go out and get what you've worked so hard for, that's all."

"I know, mom." I threw the coffee-speckled paper towel away and walked over to give my mother a kiss on the top of her fiery red-haired head. "I knew what you were saying."

My phone buzzed, and the sound of computerized ducks emerged from the back pocket of my jeans.

"What in the world is that?" My mother's face was contorted into the cutest little ball of confusion I'd ever seen.

"It's my alarm," I laughed, hoping I could stifle it just a little. I'd already sprayed coffee all over the kitchen because I was making fun of the woman who gave me life. At this point, I needed to be careful, or I was going to find myself on the wrong side of cold coffee for breakfast and peanut butter and jelly sandwiches for dinner.

"Interesting fact about coffee," I said, holding a finger in the air. "If you drink it piping hot, it's delicious. If you drink it over ice and freezing cold, it's delicious. If it's anywhere in the middle of that temperature spectrum, it is completely undrinkable."

"I don't know where that's coming from," my mother smiled. "But I'm going to go ahead and disagree with you. For my money, it doesn't get any better than a cup of coffee that was poured hot but left on the counter for a few hours. That's when things really get exciting. Just my opinion," she said, raising her eyebrows innocently.

"Really?!?" I furrowed my brow. "How can you drink that stuff?"

"I can't!" She laughed so hard at her own joke coffee almost went flying out of *her* nose. She doubled over and began slapping her thighs. "You should have seen your face!"

"Ha, ha, very funny," I said, grabbing my keys and heading for the door. "I have to get going now, or I'm going to be late."

"Okay, honey. Good luck today."

"Thanks. I'll tell you all about it over dinner."

"Sounds good. Love you."

"Love you, too."

I PARKED my car about halfway down Main Street, next to the *Coffee Creek Flour & Love Bakery*.

James was across the street and about a forty-foot walk

to the northern section of the street, right next to the *Coffee Creek Post Office*.

James Popper did not disappoint, and he hadn't even shown me any properties yet.

He was dressed to the nines in a great-looking gray suit, which, given the fact that it was almost July and temps were in the mid-eighties most days, he definitely earned some extra points in my book. His shirt was a navy blue, and he had the most enticing shade of green silk tied in a double Windsor around his neck. The whole ensemble made his thick black beard and hazel eyes really pop. He kept his head shaved really smooth on top.

He was a looker, for sure!

I wasn't sure if it was James Popper's most dapper appearance, my own excitement at finally getting my cafe started, or if the building was actually as perfect as I thought, but from the moment I saw it, I thought it was *the one*.

We hadn't even gone inside yet, and I was practically drooling over it.

The building was close to the Post Office but not connected. There was a narrow alleyway between the two buildings. The shop was narrow, with a nice little patio out front.

I was already envisioning wrought-iron tables with umbrellas and cute little chairs. This area would be able to accommodate seating for four or five people, and it would give them a wonderful view of Main Street and all of the things that were going on. It was the perfect spot for sipping coffee and people-watching while enjoying great conversation and a perfectly baked pastry.

As I brought my eyes to the building itself, the first thing that caught my attention were the two massive windows that flanked each side of the door. What a great place to have local artwork or advertise menu items that would draw people in. Plus, they were big enough that people walking by could see how inviting things were inside.

"It's perfect!" I announced to James. It was hard for me to keep from jumping up and down right there on the sidewalk.

"Well, don't you want to see it first?" He asked. "That's generally how we do things in the Real Estate business."

He held out a coffee with my name on it. I recognized Reba's handwriting and thought *girl, you're not going to be working there much longer, I promise.*

"Of course," I nodded. "I'm just a tad more than a little excited about getting started."

"I understand," he said, taking a hit off his steaming cup. "Please don't think I'm overstepping here, but it'll be to your benefit to take a deep breath and try to take the emotion out of it while you're looking. It would be a shame for you to buy a building that you were really excited about, only to find out later that it doesn't suit your needs the way you thought it would."

"That's a good point," I said, holding my cup up. "Thanks for the coffee, by the way."

"You're welcome. I didn't know what kind you liked, but the girl at the counter said you like dark roast, black as black can be. Honestly, I don't even know how she knew who I was getting coffee for."

"That's Reba," I smiled. "I told her I was meeting with you today, and she absolutely steered you in the right direction."

We stood in front of the building, drinking coffee for a moment. James was clearly in no hurry to move. It was starting to feel a bit awkward when I asked, "Are you going to show me the inside?"

"Oh, sure," he said. "I was just trying to give you the feel of what your future customers might be experiencing in this location. As you sip your coffee, look around at what's going on. Is this what you'd want for them? If it is, then maybe this is the place for you. If it's not, is there something you could do to fix it? Or would you be stuck with it as it is?"

This guy was good. I'd never thought about asking myself all of these questions. Certainly, I'd imagined my own dream scenario, but now as I looked around, I noticed a large tree that overhung the patio. I'd have to sweep leaves and acorns out of the way every day. The patio was only about ten feet from the street, and anyone sitting out there would have their view entirely blocked if a car were to park directly in front of the shop, which would inevitably happen as Main Street was crowded in the summer.

"Thank you," I said, turning to him and noticing what a punch his hazel eyes packed. "I wasn't thinking like that at all. I can definitely see some issues with this place."

"Very good. Now, we're going to go inside. I want you to think about all of the things you're going to need to set up your front of house the way you want it. Is there going to be enough counter space? Will you have enough room for patrons to be comfortable and enjoy their stay, or would you need more space? Is the kitchen area going to give you enough space for the equipment you're going to need?"

He opened the door, and I stepped into the space. At that moment, I was so thankful that God had sent James Popper to Coffee Creek. His reputation was well-earned. He didn't just want to sell me a building, make his money, and get out. It was clear that he wanted me to have the best building for me. He wanted *Connie's Cafe* to be the best it could be.

As I stepped over the threshold, I could feel a darkness about this place that I wasn't sure any amount of paint or fancy lighting would be able to fix.

"I can't thank you enough," I said. "I was ready to plunk down my money and settle into this place today. But your encouragement to look for flaws has been a real eye-opener."

"Well, we have two other places to look at today. All of

these places are going to have things you won't like. But as you look at them, start to think about which flaws you can live with and which ones are going to be too problematic to overcome."

"I will," I said, moving through the main area and into the kitchen. It was tiny and cramped, and there was no way I was going to be able to do what I wanted to do back here.

The clincher came when I looked out the back door. There was another building, big and brick, within ten feet. This meant that the only place for people to have their coffee was the patio out front or the dimly lit area inside.

This place was not the one. It's funny how slowing down for just a few minutes was enough to completely open my eyes enough to prevent me from making a major mistake.

I wrinkled my nose and looked at James. "This is not the place for me."

He nodded and gave me a wink. "Very good, grasshopper. You have mastered lesson one. Let's go see what lesson two has in store for us."

2

James and I crossed the street and started walking toward the south side of Main Street. The second property of the day was on the creek side of the street, which made me quite happy.

"I don't want to steer you or get your expectations too high, but I really think you're going to enjoy this next place a lot more than you did the first."

"We'll see," I said playfully.

"Yes," He nodded. "We will."

We were about halfway there when we passed *Coffee Creek Antiques & Valuables.* Mable Wilson, the owner, came out of the front door in a flurry.

"You've got some nerve!" She cried out. She was waving a rolled-up newspaper.

We both turned to see the seventy-five-year-old, whose wrinkles and white hair made her look much older. She was wearing a pair of loose brown pants and a knitted blue sweater, which hung on her.

"James Popper, you're going to have to answer to someone for this!"

"I'm sorry, Mable." His voice was calm, but I noticed that a few beads of sweat were forming on his forehead. "I have no idea what you're talking about?"

"I'm talking about bringing that murderer around here," she said, not mincing any words.

"Murderer?" James asked. "Mable, Connie's not a murderer. She's been proven innocent of all that stuff. She simply wants to move on with her life and start a new business in Coffee Creek. That's all."

Mable shot me a glance. "You stay right there," she said to me. "I'm warning you, don't come to a step closer." If we hadn't been in the middle of Main Street, with other people starting to get out and about for the day, I probably would have laughed a little bit at the absurdity of this whole situation. As it was, there were people starting to poke their heads out of the various shops, and this situation was not really very funny anymore … if it had ever been.

Then she opened up a newspaper from the previous month. There I was, on the front page, a horrible photo of me and a headline and article that were full of lies.

It caught me by surprise. I, honestly, thought those papers had all been thrown away.

"Mable," I said, finding my voice. "I've already been proven innocent of David Gardner's murder. It wasn't me at all."

"I don't believe that for a second." She spat on the sidewalk next to her foot. "Once a killer, always a killer." She turned her attention back to James. "And if you help her get a place down here with us honest, do-gooders, then heaven help you for what your fate may be."

James shook his head and blinked his eyes a few times, not really sure what to say to Mable.

"Mable," he finally replied. "You have a good day. I'm going to take Connie, who didn't kill anyone, by the way, to go look at another place."

He touched my arm and guided me gently. It was reassuring to have him there. I didn't know how I would have handled the exchange if it had just been me.

This is what I had been afraid of once those articles started coming out. I knew that most people would be able to understand that I hadn't done anything wrong. But I also knew that there would be others.

Unfortunately, Mable was one of those others. She had a reputation for being a rather loud gossip. Her circle was small, but they were vicious. She'd made more than a few stinks in her years, and there was one thing that I'd grown to know about Mable.

If she wanted her way, she was going to get it.

TRYING to forget the public derision at the tongue of Mable Wilson, James and I continued on to the next place on the list.

It was a tall brick building with a nice wide storefront and those big showy windows on both sides of the door.

I noticed right away that if I were to buy this building, then *Connie's Cafe* would be feet away from *Coffee Creek Reads & Teas*. I thought that this might be a very good thing. For one, tea wouldn't be on my menu. And for another, what goes better with a great book than coffee?

Nothing.

Taking a deep breath, I started to calm myself down and look around the area, taking in all of the possibilities and potential roadblocks.

The first real drawback was that I was only two doors down from that awful Mable Wilson and her antique shop. I wasn't sure that there was a place I could find that would be far enough away from her.

The second drawback I noticed was that with this building, there was no place for outside seating. The building went right up to the edge of the sidewalk, which left no room for tables and chairs as it would be in the way of people passing by, making an unpleasant experience for everyone.

"I see you looking around for outside seating capabilities," James interrupted my thoughts.

I smiled.

"That's okay," he said. "There's a surprise on the back of this building that will take care of all of your outdoor seating needs." He flashed me a grin that just about melted me.

"Ooooh", I squealed, rubbing the palms of my hands together.

Before we went in to inspect further, Rebecca Fairmack, the owner of *Coffee Creek Teas & Reads*, came out to join us.

She was a spunky little pocket of energy. She had bright blond hair, bright pink glasses, and a very chic little pastel blue dress. She was wearing orange and yellow flip-flops and drinking tea out of a mug that read: *I am a Reading & Tea Kinda Girl*. The mug had a picture of an open book and a cup of tea on the front of it.

"Hey there, Connie!" She said. Her voice was as sunny and bright as her outfit and hair. "Hi, James!"

"Hey there, Rebecca," James said. "How are things in the book and tea business going?"

She nodded, "Can't complain. People love to read and drink tea."

"That they do," James agreed. "So Connie here is going to be looking at this building here next to yours."

"Welcome to the neighborhood," Rebecca giggled.

"Thank you," I said.

Having a neighbor like Rebecca was a major positive to this second building. She was kind and upbeat, and I was already starting to think about ways that we could work together to make a really great experience for the readers and coffee drinkers of Coffee Creek.

A young couple turned into *Reads & Teas.*

"I've got to go, but we'll catch up later." She went back inside her shop. I was glad she'd come out to greet us. Her visit gave me a completely rejuvenated feeling of the Main Street vibe. I could work with her, no problem.

"Shall we," James said, bringing my focus back to the place in front of us.

"Yes," I grinned. "We shall."

THE PLACE WAS ABSOLUTELY PERFECT. The inside seating area was spacious and open, with bright hardwood floors and a nice shade of orange on the walls. This side of the street got the morning sun which made this space bright and vibrant.

The existing counters were exactly what I'd dreamt about for years. They were long and extensive, allowing for ample room for a register area, serving area, and coffee preparation area. The back counter had a great deal of space for all of the equipment, plus there was a built-in sink for quick and easy cleaning of blenders and coffee pots.

There was already a glass display case for pastries and other baked goods.

"The seller said all of the equipment in here is included in the asking price," James informed me.

"Very nice," I nodded. "I like all of this so far. I know this place is the most expensive of the three, but if I don't have to spend a ton of money on extra equipment, it might be worth shelling out a little more."

"That's what I was thinking," James flashed me that smile again, and I felt goosebumps starting on my arms. "Let's go see the kitchen."

It was a much larger kitchen than the previous place. It had full working ovens and a nice prep table in the middle, with plenty of room to move around, even if several people were back there working.

"I love this place!" I was like a child on Christmas morning, rushing downstairs and finding that Santa had brought exactly what I'd asked for. "James, I'm going to be honest with you. I don't even want to look at the third place."

He grinned. "I haven't even shown you the best part of this one yet."

I followed him out of the kitchen and back into the main area. Along the back wall there was a door that led up three steps and out onto a massive deck. There had to have been room for at least twenty tables out here. It had the most beautiful view of Coffee Creek.

The sun was glistening off the water as the birds were

flying high in the sky and the fish were jumping. I felt the warmth of the sun on my back, filling me with the happy feelings I knew my customers would someday feel when they sat out here.

"I'll take it!"

3

The *Coffee Creek Surf & Turf* was the most upscale restaurant within fifty miles of town.

On the night of the closing, my mother and Reba had insisted on taking me out for seafood and wine to celebrate the first step on the next journey of my life.

I thought that may have been a little bit over the top, but who am I to turn down buttery lobster and Chardonnay?

"I am so proud of you!" My mother's voice was almost embarrassingly loud. People from a few tables away were looking over at us and starting to stare.

"Thank you," I mumbled, turning pink. "It's really not *that* big a deal."

"Not that big a deal?" Reba joined in. "Connie, do you know what this means? You are now self-employed.

You are now a business owner, free to chart your own course through this land of the free and home of the brave!"

I nodded. "I guess when you look at it like that...."

"So, are you going to make me interview for a position? Or just hire me outright because you know me?"

"Ha, ha," I chortled through a sip of full-bodied, French oak-aged chardonnay that was every bit as buttery as the lobster that I was working on. "I think you've got the job if you want it."

She extended her hand across the table. When I shook it, she said, "I won't let ya down, boss!"

Boss.

Boy, did that feel weird. I had never been anyone's boss before. Most days, I had trouble telling myself what I was supposed to do. And now, I was going to be responsible for delegating tasks and making sure that they were done to my specifications.

It all seemed so daunting, but having Reba onboard would certainly be a helpful step in the right direction. I was sure she would coach me up if I needed it.

"So, how about after dinner, you take us to the new place?" My mother suggested. "Now that you officially have the keys, I can't think of a better way to end the evening."

"That's a great idea," Reba nodded, urging me right alongside my mother. "Let's go check it out. You can tell me where to stand." She laughed.

I nodded my agreement with the plan. "Let me just call James first and see if he would be willing to come over and give you two the fifty-cent tour."

"The fifty-cent tour," Reba giggled and elbowed my mother. "Somehow, I don't think she's calling James for us, Roberta."

"I know exactly what you mean," my mother joined in, a sly grin smeared across her face. "I haven't seen her call a boy this much since high school."

"Would you two knock it off? He's my realtor. There was a lot of communication that needed to happen to make the deal happen." I blushed as I said this, knowing that it was only half the story.

"Mmmhmmm," my mother said, rolling her eyes.

"Save it, sister," Reba joked. "We're on to you."

"Whatever," I sighed. "If you don't mind, I'm going to go make a phone call."

I stood up from the table and walked outside.

Before I pulled the phone out of my pocket to call James, Mable Wilson walked up with a small party of older women. Four of them in total, all resembling her in one form or another, from their white hair to their ambling gate. But the thing that struck me most was their vicious stares.

I heard Mable say, "That's her," as they walked by.

"The murderer?" One of the women asked, without any effort whatsoever to keep her voice down.

"In the flesh," Mable answered so I would hear every

word as clearly as could be. "Such a shame what a sham our local law enforcement is. Can't even close an open and shut case."

The five women moved into the restaurant as the hot August heat slapped my already warm face.

Don't worry about them, I told myself. *Most people know what really happened.*

I took a deep breath to gather myself and then dialed James on my phone.

It rang several times without an answer.

That's odd. He always picked up.

I hung up and tried again.

Still no answer.

Something was off.

I went back into the *Surf & Turf* and rejoined my mother and Reba, very careful not to make eye contact with Mable's miserable melee of malcontents.

"Is everything alright?" My mother asked when she saw the concern on my face.

"Trouble in paradise?" Reba joked, somewhat oblivious.

"He didn't answer his phone," I answered, then I tipped my head in Mable's direction. "Plus, she and her cronies still thought I murdered David Gardner."

"Oh, don't worry about her," my mother guffawed, slapping the air. "She's just a miserable old busybody. There's not enough drama in our quiet little town, so she and that nasty little group of Bettys are always trying to make something up to give themselves something to talk about."

"Mother?" I sat back, a little aghast. I'd known my mother was spunky but had never heard her bring out a venomous tongue like that before. "I don't know what to say right now. I've never heard you talk about another human being like that before?"

"First time for everything, I suppose." She smiled. "I'll be saying a few extra prayers of forgiveness for that, I'm sure."

"Alright," Reba said, growing tired of the prayer talk. "Let's go see this place. I'm sure you can show it to us whether James is there or not."

PUTTING the key into the doorway and turning it for the first time as the official owner of the building felt bittersweet.

I was so excited to be able to start this part of my life and share this dream with my mother. But a part of me — a big part, at that — was wishing that my father could be there to see what I was doing.

As if she could read my mind, my mother put her hands on the back of my shoulders and whispered in my ear, "Your father is very proud of you, honey. I just know he's watching you from Heaven."

It was all I could to hold back the tears as Reba, who

was oblivious to all of the emotions my mother and I were sharing, chimed in and said, "Alright, there, Connie, pop that puppy open and let us in already!"

My mother and I laughed. I quickly wiped my eyes with my palms and pushed the door open.

It was stuffy and hot inside, but that didn't stop us from storming in and looking around, dreaming about what the shop would become over the next few months.

"I want to have big chalkboards for the menus." I pointed to a spot on the walls above the back counter. "They'll be easy to hang, and we can change them up as menu items change. Plus, I think they have a lot of charm."

Reba had walked behind the counter and was pretending to write names on imaginary cups. She was putting on a show, smiling, and telling imaginary customers to have a great day.

"You have a great day," she pointed playfully. "And be sure to come back to Connie's Cafe!"

I smiled. "That sounds pretty good. You're off to a good start here. I don't want to get your hopes up, but you could very well be the first ever *Connie's Cafe Employee of the Month.*"

"Really?" She giggled, bringing her hands up to her mouth in feigned surprise. "I'd just like to thank all of the other baristas for being lazy and not nearly as friendly as me."

"You two girls are too much," my mother laughed,

looking around with a smile I hadn't seen since my father passed. "This place is absolutely perfect."

"I know," I said. "Wait until you see the deck in the back. Actually, let's go check that out now. We're probably just in time to see the sunset over the creek."

"Ooh, ooh, me first!" Reba bolted back around the counter and out the back door.

My mother put her arms around my shoulders as we were finally able to share a moment together.

"I'm so proud of you—"

Our moment was broken suddenly when we heard Reba scream.

4

I ran out to the deck, my mother following. The sun hit my eyes as I emerged from the doorway. It would have been a perfect sunset, and it would have topped off a perfect evening.

These thoughts sped through my mind quickly as my eyes adjusted to the outside light, and my ears did what they could to hold Reba's hysterics at bay while I figured out what she was so upset about.

As sunspots started to dissipate from my vision, I turned to see Reba staring and pointing toward the far corner of the deck.

There was a man sitting in a chair. His hands and feet were bound, and he had a vibrant green silk tie around his neck. His dapper dress and perfectly shiny head were snapping into focus.

Dizziness overtook me, and I dropped to the floor. A numbness that I knew all too well emerged as I slowly and methodically called 9-1-1.

"9-1-1, state your emergency," the woman on the other end of the line said robotically.

"Hello," I said, my voice as calm as possible. "I need an ambulance and the police, please."

"What is your emergency?"

"There's been a murder."

JAMES POPPER WAS DEAD.

Strangled with his own tie.

And positioned perfectly on the deck of the property I'd just purchased with his help.

"Hey, Connie," Officer Billings said when he arrived on the scene. He had come in after the paramedics. "How are you holding up?"

"Not great," I said, trying not to let my tears show.

Reba and my mother were on either side of me. We huddled together in the corner of the main area of the shop. It was dark and getting darker as the power to the building hadn't been turned on yet.

Before Billings could say anything else, one of the paramedics came over to us and informed him that the scene was now ready for the police.

"I'll be back in a bit," he said before he climbed up the steps to the deck.

My mind wandered as I thought about everything that was happening. Who would do such a thing? And why did they choose James Popper, of all people? He'd been so kind to me and helped me so much. Why had they put his body here at the shop? Had the murder occurred here? Was I going to be a suspect again? Was someone trying to send me a message?

It was almost too much to bear.

My mother pulled me close and squeezed me in a comforting way to let me know she was there. Reba's eyes were glazed over as she stared blankly off into space.

I wasn't sure how much time had passed since Officer Billings had left us to go work through the investigation, but the sun had gone down, and it was dark when he came back to us.

"Connie," he said, holding a sheet of paper out toward me. "We just found this in James Popper's pocket. Do you have any idea what it could mean?"

I unfolded the note and read: *"This is what happens when you help a murderer. She'll feel the wrath of God soon enough."*

It was hard to breathe or swallow at that moment, everything started to shut down within me, and I felt dizzy before my world went black.

"WHAT HAPPENED?" I asked, trying to sit up.

My mother was there to push me back down. "Honey, you need to relax and take slow, deep breaths."

I wasn't home. It was still dark, but I could see little beams of light coming from flashlights. They were walking by me in both directions.

Reba was on the other side of me. "You passed out," she informed me. "The paramedics were still here, so they got you onto a gurney. We're still at the shop, waiting for the police to tell us we're free to go."

"How did I pass out?" I asked.

"Don't know?" Reba shrugged. "Officer Billings handed you a sheet of paper, and after you read it, you just dropped. Honestly, you looked like you'd seen a ghost."

This brought memories swirling back. Instantly, I saw James Popper's limp head hanging at rest on his dead body; I saw the setting sun going down over the creek, perhaps, signaling the end of my dream of running the cafe before it even really began; and I saw a piece of paper that said James died because he helped a murderer.

"We have to find out who killed him," I said, sitting up.

My mother and Reba both put their hands on my shoulders, pressing me back down.

"You need to rest, honey," my mother said. "The police are working on it. They'll figure this out."

I shook my head. "It has to be me."

"I can't go through all this again," my mother pleaded. "Last time, you were threatened at gunpoint and driven through town in the trunk of a car. Enough is enough."

There was a desperation in her eyes. I knew what was behind it. I knew that she was thinking about life without both her daughter and her husband, and what that would be like. It would devastate her.

I understood what she was feeling, and I knew that her intentions were well-meaning. However, there was no way I could sit back and just let the police try to figure out who killed James Popper.

Because the murderer, whoever that may have been, was coming for me next.

5

We were finally allowed to go home around midnight. Officer Billings walked us to my mother's car, which was still parked at the *Surf & Turf*.

That late at night, there were only a few cars left in the lot, most of them belonging to employees working the closing shift. A few of them were patrons of the *Pub & Grub*, which at that time of night would have been in full swing.

"Are you ladies going to be okay to make it home?" Billings asked with genuine concern.

"We'll be just fine, Teddy," my mother smiled and rubbed my back. "Thank you for your kindness. I'm sure you have a wife and kids to go home to."

"Actually," he said, as he began rocking nervously on his heels. "It's just me."

"A handsome, honorable man like you is not married?" My mother looked at me for a moment before turning back toward him. "My, my, my. What is wrong with the young women in this town?"

Billings chuckled uncomfortably. "Thanks, Mrs. Cafe. That's really too kind."

I gave my mother a rather unsubtle shove toward her car and said, "Thanks, mom. I'm sure you can find time on a different day to call Officer Billings and have this conversation. Right now, we need to get going."

"Oh, alright," my mother said, opening the driver's side door and stepping into the car.

Reba got into the back of the car behind my mother. As I was walking around the front of the car to get into the passenger's seat, Officer Billings called to me.

"Connie?"

I stopped and looked at him.

"This is going to be different than the last time. I promise. We know you didn't do it, and we've already made a call to Detective Tolbert to come in and help. I don't know if that's going to help you rest easy, what with everything you've been through. But if it helps a little, then I'm happy for that."

"Thank you," I nodded. "I appreciate it very much."

He turned to walk away, but I had one last question for him before we called it a night.

"What do you think that piece of paper meant?"

He turned back around slowly. "Connie, I really wish I knew. It's obviously an important piece of evidence and we'll be looking at it thoroughly."

"Do you think I'm in danger? Or do you think the threat that was made was more about my soul and the afterlife?"

He shrugged. "It's hard to tell, to be honest with you. I will tell you that if you're starting to feel uneasy or unsafe about anything, you give me a call and I'll do everything in my power to make sure that nothing happens to you."

"Thanks again," I said.

When I finally sat down in my seat and buckled up, my mother was staring at me.

"Did you hear that?" She asked.

"Oh, give it a rest mom. Do you remember how we just spent our evening?"

"I'm just saying; there's never a bad time to find Mr. Right. Who knows, Connie, his name might just be Teddy. And he might just live right here in Coffee Creek."

DEAR GOD,

I don't even really know what to say right now. I guess I could start by telling you how I'm feeling.

But I don't even really know for sure what that is. I guess scared would be first.

And I know that you say in the Good Book all the time to 'Fear Not' because you're going to take care of everything for us. I'm not going to lie to you right now, though. It wouldn't do any good anyway.

The truth is, I am scared. And I'm worried about a lot of things. I'm worried mostly about my mother if anything were to happen to me. But I'm also worried that there's someone out there who wants me dead, too.

I'm confused, oh Lord, about so much right now. Was I the only reason that James Popper was killed? And if I was the reason that he was killed, does that make it my fault somehow? Or does the blame fall solely on the murderer?

Lord, I'm also wondering how many people in Coffee Creek still think I murdered that golfer, David Gardner? Because what I saw tonight didn't look like it was possible for a few old ladies who hang with Mable the antique lady to pull off. There's no way they could have overpowered James and tied him up like that. And how would they have gotten into my shop? Or did they drag him there and set him up for me, specifically to find? Did they set him up there so it would look like I did it?

The police said they weren't viewing me suspiciously, but that doesn't mean others around town won't.

I just have so much whipping around in my head. If you could give me some guidance or point me in the right direction, I would be most grateful.

And, I know this prayer has been kind of serious, God. But what in the world was my mother doing flirting with Ted Billings on my behalf? Was that all her idea? Was she exercising her good old free will in an annoying way? Or was that you speaking to me through her, trying to tell me that I'm supposed to get to know him better?

Is thirty-five too old to not have a real relationship with a man?

I just feel like so much is coming at me right now and it's all I can do to digest it. I'm afraid I'm not doing very well with it right now. But you already know that.

This much I know is true. I know, dear God, that this is all your plan. And whatever your plan is for me, I will accept it and be a force for good in this world, wherever and however I can.

Thank you for always being there. These next few days are probably going to be rough, and I might need to lean on you a lot, Lord. But I know you can handle every bit of it.

In your holy name, I pray,

AMEN

6

T he next morning, Reba stumbled down to the breakfast table, looking like she'd just woken up after a night of wild partying. Her purple hair was all over the place, sticking out in all directions, some of which I didn't even think were possible.

My mother was her usual chipper self. She stood at the coffee maker in the corner of the kitchen, dressed in a form fitting, lime green dress, and matching shoes. She had a beautiful gold chain draped nicely across her chest, and her red hair was brighter than I thought I'd ever seen it.

"Coffee ladies?" She asked cheerfully, holding up the coffee pot.

"Yes," Reba said before my mother had even finished.

"Connie?"

"Yes, please," I nodded. "I'll take some too."

"How are you doing it, Mrs. Cafe?" Reba asked, her head resting on the top of her arm, which she'd slung across the table like a kid in school trying to fall asleep during a lesson.

"I don't know," my mother said, bringing three mugs of coffee over to the table and placing them down in front of us. I think it was the only thing capable of getting Reba to sit up. "I guess I've just seen more in my life that you two, perhaps. I am very sad for that man and his family. But I've seen enough people pass away, that I know he is with the Lord, and I know that he is not suffering."

"I just can't believe it," I said, sipping the coffee my mother made. I sat back a little after I got that first jolt. My mother was smiling at me when I sent a surprised glance her way. "I knew you two would need a little high octane this morning," she winked.

"Boy, you're not kidding," Reba chimed in. "I didn't even know my name a minute ago, and now I'm ready to go climb Mount Everest."

My mother laughed. "I'm glad you like it."

We chewed our way through the coffee, devouring every drop in our mugs and refilling them once or twice just to make sure we had enough to get through the day.

"Connie, can you drive me to work after I shower?" Reba asked.

"Sure," I said. "But make it snappy, I've got things to do today."

"Like what?" My mother asked.

"Things," I said. "You know…lots of them."

She gave me a sideways glance that was definitely not approving.

Reba sensed the tension in the room and stood up. She slid along the wall slowly until she reached the doorway, at which point she ran down the hallway and up the stairs to the shower.

"Connie," my mother asked again. "What are you planning on doing today?"

"I don't want to tell you," I said, looking down and off to the side, not wanting to meet my mother's gaze.

"It's out of your hands," she warned. "Somebody else is going to have to do this work, honey. Sometimes you just need to know when to stop. Do you understand what I'm saying?"

"Yeah," I nodded. "I understand what you're saying." I brought my eyes up to meet hers. Tears had started to well up and I was on the verge of crying. "I just don't agree with it. I have to do this, mother. For me."

"How is chasing down clues in the hopes of finding a killer going to benefit you in any way?"

"They murdered James on purpose. They put him on the deck of my building on purpose. He was killed because he helped me buy that place." I walked over to the sink and started to rinse out the empty mugs. "And I'm not totally convinced they're going to stop with James."

My mother came over and stood next to me. She was

uncomfortably close, but the conversation was uncomfortable enough anyway that I didn't mention it.

"That sounds like the best reason to let the police do their jobs and find out who did this. If you really think that someone's trying to kill you, then you'd be wise to avoid snooping around."

"Mom!" I snapped. I knew I was wrong when I did it, but I couldn't help myself. I lost control for a moment.

She backed away, a defeated look on her face.

"You're right," she said, turning away, hiding her tears from me. "You're an adult, and I need to stop treating you like a child. You know how I feel. Now, it's up to you to make your own decision."

She left me alone in the kitchen and walked out the front door. I heard her car start and she was gone.

Great going, Connie.

I leaned over the sink after the mugs were clean and in the strainer to dry. Sobs came hard and heavy as I tried to piece together the last twelve hours and all that had happened.

It's one thing to find yourself in this position once, but twice in a matter of a few months. The first time was completely by accident. A very unfunny twist of fate.

This time, though, it was completely intentional, and he was targeted *because* of me.

It was almost too much to handle.

Reba showed up at the door, dressed and quasi-ready to go. Her hair was still soaking wet and dripping.

"Are you ready?" She asked.

When I stood up, and she saw my face was wet and ruddy, she said, "Oh, I'm sorry. Do you need a few minutes? You know what? I can call Dillon. He'll come get me."

"No," I said. "I'll be fine." I wiped my eyes with a tissue from a box on the counter. "Why don't you dry your hair and I'll meet you at the car in five minutes."

"It is dry," she said.

I watched the water dripping off her long hair and down one of my mother's shirts.

"I'm watching it drip all over the place."

"Oh, yeah," she said, looking down at the water rolling. "I like it like that."

I smiled. "Alright, suit yourself. Go get in the car, and I'll be out in a minute."

"Sure thing, boss," she said, giving me a quick wink, and then she left to get into the car.

I sure didn't feel like a boss at that moment, but I had to get her to work, or her current boss would be fuming at her, and her soon-to-be boss, for being late.

I took a deep breath and asked God for guidance before I left the house. I had to put my trust in Him if this was going to go anywhere at all.

I just wished He would send me a message and tell me where I was supposed to start.

fter I dropped Reba off at work, I decided to take a drive over to Main Street.

I drove past building after building, all of them in various stages of opening up their doors for another day of doing business.

Then there was my building, which still had police tape around it, denoting it as a crime scene.

I pulled my car over and parked it on the side of the road outside the future home of *Connie's Cafe* and got out.

Rebecca Fairmack was just getting *Reads & Teas* operational for the day. She came out with a folding whiteboard and positioned it in front of her store.

She crouched down in front of it and started to write the day's specials in bright red dry-erase marker.

I walked over to her, noticing her lavender dress and robin's egg-blue flats. She was one stylish woman, for sure.

"Good morning," I said softly as I approached her from behind.

She stopped writing and turned to see who was talking to her.

"Oh, hey there, Connie," she smiled and stood up, capping the marker and setting it on top of the white board. "How're you holding up? I heard about what happened last night."

"I'm doing okay," I lied.

We stood in silence for a few moments, neither one of us knowing where to go after the topic of James Popper's murder was brought up.

"Would you be okay if I went in and looked at some books?" I asked.

"Of course," she smiled. "I'm just going to finish the board, here, and I'll be right in. I can make you some tea if you'd like."

I crinkled my nose a little. "I appreciate it, but I'm more of a coffee girl, myself."

"That's right," she wagged a finger in the air. "I forgot. Well, there are loads of books on the shelves. If you like books, this place is your jam."

"Thank you," I said, and I went in.

Rebecca Fairmack had set up quite a wonderful place here in Coffee Creek. She had a narrow little shop, but she made the most of it.

The entire left-hand side was lined with bookshelves that looked as though they were built right into the building. They started at the floor and didn't stop until the ceiling, which had to have been at least twelve or fourteen feet high. Every shelf was stocked full and labeled by genre for fiction books, and topic for the non-fiction books. There was a big black, metal bar that stretched from the front of the store all the way to the back, and four sliding ladders were attached to it, making it easy for customers to read books on the top no matter where they were located along the shelves.

On the right-hand side of the shop was a small cluster of tables and chairs that would seat six or eight people comfortably. Just past these, was a little tea bar where you could walk up and order tea and scones, all of which were hand made by Ms. Fairmack, herself. Past the tea bar was another set of shelves, though these were about half the height of the shelves on the left-hand side of the store. Rebecca had hand selected some artwork that hung above these shelves, highlighting both the art itself, but also the masonry and craftsmanship of the brick walls.

Along the back wall of the shop were two large windows, which allowed ample light to enter. Rebecca had taken full advantage of the light and had set up a quaint little reading nook with comfortable high-backed chairs and a few small tables for people to use if they wanted to look at more than one book at a time.

This place was glorious and had much of the same

charm I was hoping to pull off with my place once I could get into the building and start working on it.

"Are you looking for anything specific?" Rebecca asked as she entered the shop. She walked behind the tea bar and put the marker in a drawer next to the cash register.

"Not really, Rebecca," I said. "I'm just in awe of how beautifully you've set this up."

"Well, thank you," she said, giving a little curtsy. "And please, call me Becky. My mother calls me Rebecca. I love her to death, but it's such an old-time sounding name, don't you think?"

"I guess," I shrugged. "When you put it that way, maybe? I'm sorry, I've just never given it much thought."

"Trust me," she nodded. "It makes me sound like I'm old." She moved her hands from the top of her head and down to her knees and back up again. "Be honest, do I look old?"

"No," I laughed. "You look quite young and hip."

"Exactly." She gave me a thumbs-up and came back over to where I was standing. "So, call me Becky."

"Okay...*Becky*."

We both shared a giggle for a moment before we were interrupted by the sound of a person coughing behind us.

I turned to see a small girl who was wearing a black punk rock t-shirt with chains dangling from her ripped and faded black pants. She was wearing a winter hat over her bright green hair. Her ears were lined from bottom to top with studded earrings and small hoops alike, and she had a small green gem stud in her left nostril.

"Oh, hey, Piper," Becky greeted her. She turned and pointed to me. "Do you know Connie Cafe? She's going to be our neighbor next door." Then Becky turned to me and said, "Connie, this is Piper. Piper's in high school. She works here in the summer, stocking books and helping customers when we get busy."

"Nice to meet you," I said. I stepped forward and offered my hand.

Piper looked at it for a minute, seemingly not sure what to do. Then she put her fingertips in my palm and moved them up and down before pulling them back quickly.

"Nice to meet you," she said, looking down at the ground.

"Piper, there's a new shipment of books that came this morning. Please check them in, mark them and shelve them where they'll fit. Work any extras into displays that have gaps. If there are any books left after that, come get me, and I'll help you place them in the store room."

Piper nodded and then slinked past Becky and through a little door that was just past the tea bar.

"She's come a long way, believe it or not," Becky said once Piper was out of earshot. "I would have never hired her if it was entirely my decision, but she's my brother's kid, and he asked if she could have a job for the summer. That was two months ago." Becky looked over her shoulder to make sure Piper was out of earshot. "Between you and me, I'll be glad when school's back in session."

I made a motion like I was zipping my lips shut. "My lips are sealed. Your secret is safe with me."

"So, do you know when you'll be able to get in next door and open things up?" Becky asked as I made my way through the store, browsing her selection of books.

"I have no idea. I'm hoping sooner than later. As it is, I feel like I'm getting a pretty late jump on things. I'd really wanted to be opened by now, but now I'm thinking I might be able to open sometime in the early fall. Just in time for pumpkin spice season." I gave a thumbs-up that was less than genuine.

"I know what you mean," Becky nodded. "I'm the same way with tea. It's a shame more people don't appreciate it for what it is on its own. I'm not a big coffee drinker, but I have to believe that there's probably enough subtlety and nuance with the beans and roasting methods that covering it with all that sugar defeats all of the work that went into getting the bean to the point where it could become coffee."

"Exactly," I agreed. "My father always drank his coffee black. He would sit with me on the porch and talk to me over and over again about appreciating the simple things in life because the beauty is in the simplicity."

"Yes," Becky nodded. "One hundred percent, yes! I won't bore you, but it's the same way with tea leaves. It is an absolute miracle that something so wonderful and simple and pleasureful exists that we are doing it a disservice to dump sugar and milk, and goodness knows what other kind of chemicals, into it."

"Aunt Becky," Piper called, emerging from the back room. "I can't find the check-in sheet."

I saw Becky turn slightly away from Piper and roll her eyes and take a deep breath before she answered. "Okay, Piper, I'll be right there. Why don't you work on taking all of the books out of the box while you wait."

"I did already," Piper said.

"I'll let you go," I smiled at Becky. "We'll chat again soon," I said. "After all, in a few days, once all that police tape is removed, we'll officially be neighbors."

"Very true," Becky nodded. "I'm looking forward to it."

Becky turned and followed Piper into the back room. I took my leave and walked back out onto Main Street, feeling a little more hopeful than I had twenty minutes earlier.

8

Walking back up Main Street, I felt a slightly renewed sense of purpose and determination. I was going to find out who killed James Popper, and nothing was going to stand in my way.

I thought the best place to start might be *Coffee Creek Realty*, which was located at the North end of Main Street, on the same side as *Reads & Teas*.

Unfortunately, it was also on the same side of the street as Mable's *Antiques & Valuables*.

The thought of walking by that shop gave me an uneasy feeling and a lump in my throat. There was something about that woman, even though she was old and hunched over and physically feeble, that just made me feel weak in comparison.

As I approached her store, I felt my heart start to pound harder and faster in my chest. I picked up the pace of my walk, hoping that maybe, I could walk past her place undetected.

"Murderer!" Mable's voice broke through the sound of my beating heart.

Just keep going, I told myself. *Ignore her, for she knows not what she does.*

"That's right!" Mable shouted. I was already past her shop, but she was out on the sidewalk, yelling at me from behind. "Keep on walking, just like the cowardly killer you are!"

My face was flush from embarrassment, plus the extra energy I'd put into walking as fast as I could.

By the time I reached the realty offices, a number of people had come out of their shops to catch a glimpse of who Mable was yelling at.

"Pipe down, you old bat!" I heard a voice that made me smile. It came from the Post Office. Martin Welker was heading out for his usual route. He was just getting into his truck when he uttered those words in my defense.

I would never call anyone an *old bat*, but I couldn't stop myself from silently cheering him on as he let Mable have what was coming her way.

"Go back inside and sell some old stuff," he continued. "And leave that poor girl alone, or I'm going to call the cops and have them cite you for noise pollution."

"I'd like to see you try," Mable said. "Remember, you've got skeletons in your closet, too!"

Martin just shook his head and started the engine of his postal truck. "You're a real beauty," he called out over the rumble of his vehicle. "I'm sure the Devil's making a nice warm spot for you as we speak!"

"Why, I never...." Mable, for once, was rendered speechless.

Martin pulled out of the Post Office parking lot, squealing his tires as he set off on his route, whipped up into some kind of frenzy.

Before I opened the door to the realty offices, I took one last look at Mable, who was now directing every ounce of her anger through her eyes in my direction. "You're still a murderer! And nobody will ever get me to shut up about that!"

I waited for a moment, hoping that she would go back into the antique store. But she wasn't going to allow me to have that satisfaction. Rather, she stood in the center of the sidewalk, her eyes unwavering.

I closed my eyes and took a deep breath, and turned the doorknob to go into the offices and talk to someone who knew more than I did about James Popper.

COFFEE CREEK REALTY was a small office, no bigger than someone's living room.

There were three desks inside. Fluorescent lighting in the ceiling gave it a bright feeling.

I thought it a bit odd that one of the three realtors had been murdered the night before, yet the two who were remaining were going about their days as though it was business as usual.

"May I help you?" A youngish-looking woman, perhaps in her late twenties, looked up from her desk. She was dressed in a navy suit with a white blouse. The nameplate in front of her said her name was Tiffany Elizabeth.

"Hi," I said, stepping into the building a little further. "I'm Connie Cafe. I was just...well....I'm..." What exactly was I there to do?

I stumbled over my words for a minute until the man, whose nameplate said was Matthew Grant, stood up and walked over to me.

"You were working with James, weren't you?" He asked. His voice was soft and conciliatory.

"Yes," I nodded solemnly. "I very much enjoyed the process of working with him. I'm shocked that he's gone."

"We are, too," said Tiffany. "I mean, just yesterday, we were joking around about what a crank Mable was and how much commission he was getting off your place. And the next thing you know...."

Her voice trailed off, and her face went blank.

"I know," I said, nodding. "It's quite shocking and sad. I really liked him. He seemed like a really great guy."

"He was excellent," Matthew agreed. "By far the best realtor for miles around. He could sell anything. I wish I was able to close deals the way he did."

"Well, he certainly made it easy for me to buy," I said.

"So, is there anything we can help you with?" Tiffany asked again.

"Oh," I stammered. "I guess not. I was just stopping in to see how everyone here was doing, I guess."

"Yeah, thanks for that." Tiffany stood up and walked me to the door. "I really don't want to be rude, but it's definitely a little more stressful around here without James to help with some of the load. Plus, we have to redo a bunch of paperwork to make sure his commissions get taken care of properly."

I nodded. "That must be incredibly difficult having to focus on your job after someone you were close to was...." I couldn't bring myself to say *murdered*.

Tiffany's eyes met mine, and she conveyed her understanding through a subtle tip of her head. I was thankful that she understood what I was saying without having to actually say it.

"If you need anything else," Matthew called out, "don't hesitate to stop by or give us a call."

"Thank you," I said, stepping back out onto the sidewalk, but I doubt very much that they heard me because the door shut quickly behind me.

"Murderer!"

Mable had not gone inside yet.

She'd waited for me the entire time.

It was going to be a great pleasure having a business down the street from her.

She's a real peach.

9

Just after four, I picked Reba up from her shift and drove her home.

Dillon was just pulling into the driveway.

Up until this point, I had still not met him. He seemed to be a very busy fella. Every time that Reba and I had gotten together at her place, he was either out of town on a business trip or visiting his parents a few towns over.

Now that I was finally able to lay eyes on the man, it was shocking just how different the two were from one another.

Reba had purple hair that she put in many different styles. Dillon had blond hair that was cut short into a crew cut. Reba wore bright, colorful outfits that matched her hair and eyes. Dillon wore a black suit with a navy blue tie that also matched his hair and eyes.

These things, aside from what Reba'd already told me, made it clear that the expression *Opposites Attract* was more than just a catchy phrase.

He walked from his car to mine. I rolled down the window.

"You must be Connie," he said, flashing me a bright white grin. "Reba's told me so much about you."

"You must be Dillon. I have to admit, you're still a bit of a mystery to me, but Reba says that you are a very good cleaner."

He blushed a little, nodding his head and laughing. "That's me," he admitted. "I've always been a little more feminine than my father thought I should be. But it's paying off. I found a great woman like Reba because of it."

"Awww, thanks, hon!" Reba called across my body and out the driver's side window. "Listen, Connie, and I gotta have a little bit of a pow-wow. Could you do me a favor and go inside and get the kitchen clean so I can make you dinner?"

"Whatever you say," he winked. He then must've realized that I was still there and watching them because he said, "Oh, I'm sorry. That wink was for Reba."

"I know."

"It was nice to meet you, Connie," he waved and then turned and walked up the deck and into the top-level apartment.

"You have no idea how lucky you are, do you?" I asked, turning to Reba.

"Yeah," Reba nodded. "He's alright. I'll probably hang onto him for a while."

"So listen," I changed the subject. "I wanna solve this murder. Do you think that we can meet up and write some stuff down on the elephant poop paper?"

"Well, after what you did the last time, there's no way I'm helping you out at all. I'm not ready to die, or be held at gunpoint, or go for a joyride in someone else's trunk, but…hold on a minute!" Reba smiled a devilish grin.

She got out of the car and walked up into the apartment. As she opened the door, I heard her yell to Dillon, "If you don't get it clean, you don't eat! It's that simple buster!"

I laughed and thought *she'd better be careful.*

A few minutes later, she emerged, holding something behind her back and grinning like the Cheshire Cat.

"I've been saving these for you. I was going to wait until Christmas, but seeing as how we're still like six months away, I'm just going to give them to you now."

She brought her hands in front of her and displayed two brand new poop paper notebooks.

"You shouldn't have," I smiled. "You know, I do have a yellow legal pad at home. I would have just used those."

"Oh," she said, making a face as she'd just lost her best friend. "But you said you wanted poop paper. Look, this one's elephant…but this other one's sloth. Very rare."

I held out my hand and took the notebooks from her.

"Thank you. I'll cherish them for the rest of my life."

That was enough to get Reba to smile.

"You'd better go inside and give that man of yours some love for all the work he's doing."

"Maybe," she shrugged. "I'm pretty tired. I'll probably just put on some sweatpants and watch TV while he cleans up the kitchen."

"Alright," I said. "So, what are you cooking for dinner?"

"I dunno," she shrugged. "It's feeling like a frozen pizza kinda night."

I laughed. She was such a go-getter, that one.

She turned to head back inside, and I stared at the poop paper notebooks on the front seat. I was honored to have this new found paper supply, but what I really wanted was Reba's help.

But at this point, that seemed like a step too far.

WHEN I ARRIVED HOME, the house smelled of peanut butter cookies.

My mother had been in the kitchen for the better part of two hours baking like a mad woman. When I walked into the kitchen, she was wearing her famous cookie-making apron. It had a picture of a gingerbread man on it. Surrounding him was the phrase, *Let's Get Baked*.

Someone had given it to my mother a while back for her birthday. She thought it was super funny, and the gingerbread man had the most adorable little face. But I still don't think she knows exactly what it means.

Then again, maybe a part of me just didn't want her to be so worldly.

"Hey, mom," I said, walking into the kitchen and grabbing a peanut butter cookie off a plate. Before I could get it up to my mouth, she slapped my hand with a nearby spatula.

"Those aren't for you!"

I dropped the cookie back onto the plate and looked around, noticing that there were three different types of cookies on about ten different plates, all around the counter.

"Who are they for then?" I asked, my mouth agape.

"Let's just say we're going to go pursue a lead," she winked.

AN HOUR LATER, we were pulling up to the *Coffee Creek Police Station* with a backseat full of cookies on plates wrapped in cellophane.

"You've got to be kidding me," I said, hiding my head in my hands.

"I most certainly am not kidding you," my mother glared at me. "I spent all afternoon making cookies to thank Officer Billings and his crew for their help last night. The least you could do is get out of this car and put a smile on your face while we deliver them."

I sighed deeply.

"Oh, come on, Connie. What are you waiting for? You heard him the other night. He's not married. Plus, he's a very honorable man and handsome too."

"I know, mom. He's handsome and sweet and single. I get it."

"I bet you he treats his mother with respect. That's important in a man, you know. If he treats his mother well, he'll treat his wife well, too."

"Don't you think you're getting a little ahead of yourself?" I asked, in complete disbelief that I was having this conversation with my mother.

"You have to look ahead a little, Connie. You can't just keep flying by the seat of your pants. That's how you end up old and alone. And let's face it, that's not what the Lord wants for us."

I nodded. I knew she was right. I hated that she was right.

I threw open the car door and stepped outside, looking more like a seventeen-year-old than the grown woman I purported to be.

"Watch and learn," she smiled. "You grab those macarons, and I'll get these peanut butter guys."

"But that's only two plates?"

"Just watch and learn," she repeated.

I followed her inside the police station. I didn't know how often she did this, but it was clear by everyone's reaction that it had happened more than a few times before.

"Hey, everyone!" Officer West called out. He was standing at the usually vacant receptionist desk. "Roberta's back with more goodies!"

I looked at my mother, shocked that even Donald West knew her by name.

There were four or five other officers that came over and thanked us as we set the plates down on the desk.

"You boys know the drill," my mother smiled coyly.

To my surprise, they all barreled past us and out to our car.

"That's how it's done," Roberta Cafe winked at me.

Officer Billings was a little late to the party and came around the corner from his office a moment later.

"Oh, hey Connie...Mrs. Cafe."

"Hello, Teddy," my mother said. "Connie made cookies for everyone."

I shot her a quick glance. I was not liking where this was going all of a sudden. Not that I had been too hot on its trajectory before.

"Really?" Officer Billings smiled. He stared at me with his baby blues. And even in my embarrassment and retro-teenage angst, I felt attracted to his handsome face and kind smile.

I also didn't want to tell a lie, so I just smiled and said nothing.

"Thanks," he said. "We love our cookies around here."

"We know," my mother chimed in, patting me on the back. "Say, Teddy, do you have a moment to talk in private?"

"Sure," he said, "why don't you two follow me back to my office."

He turned, and we followed my mother, grabbing my wrist and dragging me the whole way. I gave about as much of a fight as I could without making it too obvious to any onlookers — of which there were none, now that my mother had trapped them all with freshly baked cookies — that I was being dragged against my will.

Once we were in Officer Billings's office, he invited us to sit down. My mother did not sit down.

Neither did I.

"This won't take long, Teddy."

"Okay," he nodded, looking a little confused.

"You and Connie went to school together, right?"

He nodded.

"She's a pretty girl, right?"

He looked at me, and I could tell when our eyes met that he was just as mortified as I was.

"Why don't you take her to dinner sometime?"

"Mom?!?"

She waved my protest away with her hand. "I'm serious. I'm tired of watching my young, attractive, intelligent daughter and this wonderful young, attractive, honorable man go through life alone."

Officer Billings looked at me and then brought his attention back to my mother.

"Roberta...Mrs. Cafe...that's very nice of you, and I'm honored and all, but I could never take Connie out if she didn't want to go with me. That would be wrong."

My mother shot me a quick elbow in the rib. "Tell him, Connie, that you'd love to go out with him."

My mother was staring at me.

Officer Billings was staring at me.

My father, God, and the Sweet Baby Jesus were staring at me from on high — I was sure of it.

I shrugged.

"Sure?"

10

It just so happened that Officer Billings's shift ended twenty minutes after my mother had asked him out for me.

And since he didn't have a family to worry about, he changed clothes at the office and we ended up going out for a night on the town right then and there.

I, honestly, don't know what would have been worse in that situation: Going home with my mother and having to wait for a date I wasn't sure I wanted, or watching my mother walk out of the police station without me and not waiting at all for a date I wasn't sure I wanted.

"So, where would you like to go?" He asked, meeting me out in the parking lot. He was dressed in a cobalt blue polo and a pair of khaki shorts.

"I don't know," I said, nervously. "I really wasn't planning on this tonight."

"Me either," he chuckled. "Your mother is quite a firecracker, isn't she?"

I nodded. "That she is."

I smiled and looked him in the eyes, and as weird as this all was, I felt suddenly at peace with the idea. I could tell he had a gentle soul. My mother had seen it before I had. But, at this moment, I knew the night was going to be alright.

Ted Billings drove a big truck. Getting in and out was a challenge for me, as I was much shorter than him. He helped me in and drove us to the end of Main Street.

Putting the truck in park, he said, "Do you want to just take a walk and see where that leads us?"

"That sounds really good," I smiled. "Let's do that."

We walked down Main Street talking about the impact that growing up in Coffee Creek had on us.

"I love it here," he said. "I can't imagine living anywhere else. This place is my home, through and through."

"My idea of Coffee Creek is a little different than yours," I said. "I love it here, don't get me wrong. But I was on a path that was taking me away from here before my father died. That was fourteen years ago, and I'm still here. I often wrestle with God about my path. I'm constantly questioning whether or not this is where I truly belong."

"I can see that," he nodded. "So, what's He saying to you lately?"

"Lately," I guffawed. "Lately, he has definitely been sending me the *Get Out of Dodge* messages."

"How so?"

"Well, let's just recap the past four months. I've found two dead bodies, one of which was found in the building where I am going to put my coffee shop. I've been a suspect in a murder investigation, and terrible things were written about me in the paper I worked on for years by people that I thought were my friends. I took a ride in a guy's trunk and thought for sure that I was going to die. Oh, and my mother asked a cop out on a date for me. In the prayer world, those are what one might call *signs*."

We shared a quick laugh about things before he gave his take on the situation.

"You know, Connie, I don't claim to know what God's plan is for myself, let alone anyone else. But the way I look at it, without those things happening, you and I wouldn't be here talking like this tonight."

I hadn't thought about it that way. I'd just felt all of the unpleasantness of everything that had occurred over the last little while. But he was right. If I hadn't found David Gardner's body, taken a ride in the trunk of a car, and had my mother overstep big time, I might have missed out on the moment I was currently in.

"I don't know if you're right," I smiled, "but you do have a point."

We walked up and down Main Street talking for hours without ever going anywhere. We didn't have dinner, and that was alright with me.

Mable had gone home for the night. That was definitely okay with me.

Ted brought me home and walked me to the front porch.

"I had a great time tonight," he said.

I smiled. "Me too."

Both of us stood there, unmoving in the darkness. I didn't want to go in, and I could tell that he was in no rush for the night to end either.

Finally, he said, "Should we do this again sometime?"

"What?" I joked. "Stare awkwardly at each other on my front porch."

He laughed and shook his head. "No. I mean, should we—"

"I know what you mean," I giggled. "And the answer is yes."

"Sounds great," he nodded. "I will see you later then. Thank you for a wonderful evening."

"You too," I said, waving and turning to go inside.

I waited just inside the front door as he pulled his truck out into the road and drove back into town.

I stood there until his taillights were out of view. Then I headed up to my room.

When I reached the top of the stairs, I saw my mother's bedroom light click off.

I smiled.

She was right.

I found myself thinking that I should listen to her more often.

11

"So, how did things go with Mr. Wonderful?" My mother smirked as she handed me a tall mug of my morning medicine.

"Mr. Wonderful?" I laughed. "Don't you think it's a tad early to be donning him with that moniker?"

"I don't know," she batted her eyelashes. "Is it?"

"Maybe, a little," I said, bringing my finger and thumb about an inch together and crinkling my nose.

"I don't know," she smiled. "You two were out for a pretty long time last night. That's all I'm saying." She took a sip of her coffee. "Where I'm from, that's called success."

I rolled my eyes. "Oh, jeepers."

"What? I'm serious."

"I know you are," I nodded, taking my first sip. "That's what scares me."

"So, what did you two do? Did he take you out to dinner?"

"No."

"A show?"

"No."

"Shopping?"

"Nope, none of those." I smiled, knowing that *not* knowing was starting to drive her nuts.

"Well, come on, then. Out with it!"

"We just walked and talked."

"Oh, honey," she said, sitting back in her chair and putting her mug down on the table. She clasped her hands together and brought them up to her mouth.

"What?" I scoffed. "It's nothing."

"Oh, but it is," she said. "I don't want to put too many thoughts in your head. But that was exactly what your father and I did on our first date. We walked that same street as you and Teddy, just talking, not a care in the world about who or what was around us."

I sat back and tried to take it all in.

"Mom?" I asked. "Did you ever think you were in the wrong place?"

"What do you mean?" She asked, picking up her coffee and sitting back in her chair.

"I don't know," I said, staring past her, trying to figure out how to put my feelings into words. "I guess it just feels like God might be pointing me in a different direction, you know? With all the murder and things that seem to keep happening."

She nodded. "I understand."

"You do?"

"Yes." She sat forward and put her hand on top of mine. "And I would strongly advise you to stay the course and continue to pray. The answer for you will come when you least expect it."

"Are you sure?"

"No," she shook her head. "Just telling you what's worked for me over the years. We can never be sure. That's why what we have is called faith. It's a belief in the unknown, the uncertain. It's choosing to follow something we can't see, trusting that He's going to guide us and help us come to the right conclusions."

"Have you ever had trouble trusting?"

"Oh, heavens, yes." She laughed and put her empty coffee cup down on the table. "You know, after your father died, I didn't want to live anymore. I had no idea what I was supposed to do with my life. You were here to help, and that was great, but I was lost and broken. And I'll tell you, God and I had more than a few late-night wrestling matches."

"So, what changed everything?"

She sat back and thought for a minute. "I think it was just taking things one step at a time. Weathering tough storms can be tremendously difficult, but if you keep putting one foot in front of the other, eventually, you find yourself on dry land and out in the clear. God guides us all and shows us the way when we are ready to see it. Trust me, honey. Just keep putting one foot forward. You'll find where you're supposed to be eventually."

I nodded.

I knew she was right. "It's just hard to see through the clouds sometimes."

"I understand," she said. "But it seems to me that, perhaps, those clouds broke a little last night. Right?"

She raised her eyebrows and gave me a pat on the knee.

"Think about it," she whispered in my ear.

Dear God,

First off, I want to say thank you for giving me the most amazing mother ever. She is so full of life and wisdom and spunk and all of it.

I don't have to tell you this, but I was completely mortified yesterday when she asked Ted Billings to take me out. I didn't know what to do, and I'm not going to lie — I was cursing your name a little bit inside my head. But, again, you already knew that.

As it turns out, spending time with Ted was a really great thing. I hope it was great for both of us, but I know it was definitely something that I enjoyed tremendously.

Now, on to the hard stuff, oh Lord.

I know there's a reason James Popper was put in my building to discover. And I know there's a reason that I discovered him. I just don't know why.

Perhaps, it's because I am supposed to give up my dream of running Connie's Cafe. But I don't think that's it. I don't think you would put me in the place I was only to pull the rug out from beneath my feet.

No.

There has to be a different reason.

I just don't know what that reason is…yet.

I have no doubt with your guidance that, I will find out the reason eventually. But Lord, if it's at all possible, feel free to send me a sign. Something I can see, or touch, or feel. It's really hard to go at these things blind. I don't have enough wisdom within me to know what you want me to do.

Am I supposed to get involved with this? Am I supposed to start making notes and tracking down leads, and figuring out the puzzle of it all?

Or did I do it wrong that last time? Are you giving me a redo? Are you trying to tell me that I wasn't supposed to find David Gardner's killer? But I did. And that's why you've put James Popper in front of me? As a test. Do you want me to just sit back, oh Lord, and let the police do their work?

Even praying that doesn't sound right? It doesn't sound like your ways to hurt a child of God simply to teach me a lesson. Perhaps, my vision is too narrow, God. Perhaps, I need to broaden my lens and look at this a different way.

Maybe James Popper was killed as a result of evil motives, and you are using me as your instrument to help in some way. Am I supposed to help rid this town of some evil among us?

I wish I knew, and I wish you would reveal your plan to me a little quicker than you are.

But everything in your time, not mine.

Thank you, Lord, for all of the many blessings in my life. And thank you, Lord, for the path that you will, no doubt, reveal to me as I move forward through this very confusing time in my life.

In your holy name, I pray,

AMEN

12

It was mid-morning on the third day since the murder of James Popper, and I was all business.

I called up the police station and asked to speak with Ted.

"Hey, you," he said, his voice playful on the other end of the line.

"Hey," I said. "Listen, I don't want to be dismissive or anything. I had a really great time last night. But I need to know if I can get back into my shop or not?"

"Sure, let me check on the progress of the investigation so far."

He put me on hold and a very cheerful message about *The Coffee Creek Police Department* and their dedication to every citizen in the community began playing in my ear. I had to listen to it play three times through before Ted was back on the line. To be fair, it was only about twenty seconds long.

"Connie?"

"Yup, I'm here."

"So, everything that we needed to do in there has been done. I'm sending over Officer Freeman now to remove all of the police tape so you can get inside."

"Great," I said, "Thanks."

"No problem. Quick question."

"Sure."

"Are you planning on heading over there anytime soon?"

"Yes," I said, grabbing my purse and keys and walking out to my car. "I'm heading over right now."

"Okay, great. I'll have Officer Freeman stay with you for a little while to…you know…."

"What?" I asked. "What do I know?"

"Well, I'm just concerned for your safety, given the note that we found in Mr. Popper's pocket the other night."

I sighed. "I appreciate your concern Ted, but trust me, I'll be just fine."

"At the risk of sounding a little too bold and possibly ruining the sentiments of last evening, I have to share this with you. I am not aware of many people, if any, who thought they were going to be in danger before danger showed up. Everyone thinks they're going to be fine…until they aren't."

I smiled. "First, I *am* going to be fine. Second, I think it's sweet that you want to protect me. And third, you did not ruin any sentiments of last evening."

"Great! Are you going to be working in the shop all day today?"

"I don't know. Why do you ask?"

"Well, I get off work at five. I was wondering if you'd like me to pick you up and we could have another evening together. This time, I'd take you out to dinner."

"Well, that sounds lovely. But why don't you pick me up at my place? I'm going to need time to shower and get ready if we're going to have dinner."

"Sounds great. I'll see you then. Officer Freeman just left in a squad car. He should be over at your place in a few minutes."

"That'll be perfect timing."

As I WALKED UP to the shop, it was refreshing to see that the yellow police tape had been removed from the front steps and doorway.

I stood there staring at the front of the building, excited about the prospect of getting started on real work toward my dream.

"Murderer!"

That didn't take long.

Mable was out in front of her store, screaming at me at the top of her lungs.

I turned and waved to her. "Good morning, Mable."

Before I went inside I took a second to survey the street and see who was witnessing the harassment coming my way.

Much to my surprise, it was only Piper, whose hair was now a very fake shade of yellow. She was on her way into *Reads & Teas*, and she was staring at me as Mable continued her verbal barrage.

As soon as I made eye contact with her, she put her head down, stared at the sidewalk, and quickly ducked inside the bookstore.

What a strange child, I thought to myself.

With a shrug, I went to enter my shop.

At first, I was surprised that the door was open slightly. But then I remembered that Ted had sent Officer Freeman over to protect me.

I pushed the door open and listened for his presence. It was silent in the main shop area.

"Officer Freeman?" I called out.

There was no answer. I went back into the kitchen and called out again. "Officer Freeman?"

This was starting to freak me out a little. Ted said he was sending him over, the police tape was removed, and my door was open — but there appeared to be no Officer Freeman.

Ted's words rang loud in my ears as I began up the

steps toward the deck: *Everyone thinks they're going to be fine... until they aren't.*

As I stepped out onto the deck, those words, along with Mable's cries of *Murderer,* were ringing in my head.

A pit formed in my stomach as I saw Officer Freeman for the first time. He had a crumpled-up wad of police tape in his hand. He was lying facedown on the deck in the corner where James Popper had been discovered. He had two bullet holes in his back, and a note had been taped on him. Written in red marker were the words, *Murderers have a special place in Hell.*

THE SIRENS on the squad cars were deafening as they came roaring around the corner onto Main Street. Their blue and red lights could be seen from a distance as they grew closer.

Ted got out of the first car and came running up the front steps toward me. Detective Tolbert followed as closely as his age would allow. I hadn't seen Detective William Tolbert in a few months, as he left town after the David Gardner murder was solved. Ted told me that they called him back in to help with the James Popper murder. Thankfully, he had arrived.

"Are you alright?" Ted asked, wrapping me up in his arms, without a care in the world that anybody saw.

"I think so," I said, settling into the embrace, allowing the tears to come freely.

"Go check on Freeman," he ordered the other officers as they reached the entryway.

Detective Tolbert stood in the wings, waiting for his opportunity, giving Ted a rather dismissive look.

Ted finally let go of me and looked at Tolbert.

"That's rather unorthodox police work, Billings," Detective Tolbert frowned.

"It's a little complicated," Ted blushed.

"It must be," Tolbert replied, stepping in to ask me questions.

"Ms. Cafe," he said, extending his hand for a formal shake. "Please, don't hold it against me if I don't give you a hug," he shot a look at Ted. "I'm just not the hugging type."

A fake grin emerged beneath his bushy mustache.

"So, Connie…may I call you Connie?"

"Yes," I nodded.

"Thank you. After all, it seems only fitting with the amount of time we're spending together lately. Just like old friends," he shot another glance at Ted. "Only, a tad more professional."

There was an awkward silence among the three of us before he continued.

"It seems like this is becoming commonplace for you, yes?"

"Unfortunately," I agreed.

"I've been briefed on the murder of James Popper and made aware of the note that was in his pocket at the time of his death. Is there anything you wish to add to the existing information?"

I shrugged. "I don't know. To be quite honest with you, I'm in a fair bit of shock. James's murder was one thing, and the note attaching the motive to fear or hatred of myself was another. But this last thing…he was a police officer. I don't even know what to think now. It seems like nobody's safe."

Detective Tolbert nodded, "It does appear as though someone is certainly trying to scare you, and the rest of us who would have anything to do with you, in the process."

At that moment, one of the officers that had been sent out to the deck came rushing into the main room where we were talking.

"He's alive!" He shouted. "We need to get the paramedics here ASAP!"

"I UNDERSTAND," Ted said, finishing up on the phone. We were still standing around the main area of what might someday be Connie's Cafe. "That's very good news. Thank you…alright, goodbye."

He turned and looked at Detective Tolbert and me. "Office Freeman's going to be okay. The bullets missed his internal organs. He'll be on the mend for a while, but he's going to live."

I breathed a deep breath of thanks.

"That's good news, Billings," Detective Tolbert nodded. He turned to me and said, "Ms. Cafe, in light of recent events, we are going to keep your building closed down for the foreseeable future."

I nodded that I understood. But I was devastated on the inside. I didn't dare show any emotion in front of Ted or Detective Tolbert. I'd save that for home. But I was a ball of emotion. How many more people were going to die because they knew me? How many murderers were there in Coffee Creek? Would it ever be safe for me to come back here again?

I had no idea what the future held, and at that moment, it seemed like God was playing a cruel game with me. I knew deep down that that wasn't the case. But, boy, did it feel that way.

"Should I set up a security detail for Connie? Someone to keep an eye on her house and follow her and her mother around for a while?" Ted asked.

Detective Tolbert shook his head, sending another sharp look in Ted's direction. "No, that won't be necessary at this time. Not to mention, you're going to be down a man for the next little while. Your resources seem to be spread thin enough as it is."

"What do you suggest we do to keep Connie and her mother safe?" His voice had a protective edge to it that I found sweet. At the same time, I knew if he didn't cool it, he was going to find himself in more trouble than this was probably worth.

"I suggest we get to work, roll up our sleeves, and find out who killed James Popper and who attempted to kill Officer Freeman. That's what I suggest."

With that, Detective Tolbert walked out the front door and drove away.

"Sorry," Ted shrugged. "I tried. He just doesn't seem to understand."

"I think it's sweet that you want to keep me safe," I smiled. "But do me a favor, would you?"

"What?"

"Don't do anything stupid because you're thinking too much of me and not enough of your job."

"Don't worry about that," he assured me. "I'll be fine."

"You know," I said, "a wise man once told me, *Everyone thinks they're going to be fine...until they aren't.*"

"Touche," he smiled. "Touche."

13

After a simple dinner with my mother (baked tilapia, steamed broccoli, and roasted potatoes with caramelized onions seasoned with garlic, salt and pepper, and a glass of ice water with a lemon to drink), I headed up to my bedroom to begin the process of figuring out who in the world was tormenting me and attempting to kill people who were trying to help me.

My mother knocked on the door a few minutes after I'd settled onto my bed with my yellow legal pad. I still couldn't bring myself to use Reba's poop paper notebooks.

"I noticed you were pretty quiet at dinner," she said, poking her head into the room. "Is everything alright?"

I didn't know what to say, or how to answer her. I really wasn't in much of a hurry to start unpacking everything right now. I felt like I was already behind on this mystery and just wanted to get to the bottom of it already. But I also knew that shutting my mother out and keeping her at a distance wasn't going to help, either.

"I'm going to be okay," I replied. "I'm just not that great right now."

"Are you still trying to figure out the James Popper murder?"

I nodded. She still hadn't heard about Officer Freeman. That news was still pretty new and hadn't made it to her circles of information as of yet.

"There was an attempted murder at the shop today," I told her. "That's where I was all afternoon."

"Oh, my," she said, covering her mouth with her hand and entering my room. She sat down on the edge of my bed. "Who was it?"

"Officer Freeman," I told her.

"What a shame," she shook her head. "I like him so much."

"They said he's going to be okay, but it's going to be a while. He was shot twice in the back out on the deck. Mom, he was in the exact same spot that James Popper was."

I started to sob.

My mother wrapped her warm, loving arms around me. "There, there," she said, running her hand over my hair. "I'm here for you."

"I know." I attempted to nod, but she had a sturdy hold on my head. "You've always been there when I needed you."

She finally let go, and I brought my head up, thankful for a few deep breaths of fresh air.

"Have you talked to Ted about this?"

"Of course," I said, flashing her a look. "He was there with me all afternoon."

"That's nice. At least he's aware of everything."

"I'm not so sure," I shook my head. "I'm worried that his newfound interest in me might be clouding his judgment just a little."

"What do you mean?"

"Well, he's a little overprotective all of the sudden, and he was a titch less than professional today at the crime scene. Mom, he hugged me in front of Detective Tolbert."

"Who's Detective Tolbert again?"

"He was the guy that helped with the David Gardner investigation a few months back."

"Is he the one that came up with that idiotic idea where you had to wear a wire?"

"That's the guy."

"Ooh, I don't like him," she said, crinkling up her face. "He put my baby in harm's way."

"I was fine."

"You could have *died*! I would not call that fine."

She had a point. But to be fair to Detective Tolbert, I

had been the one to go to him with evidence. He was just the one that figured out a way that I could help without getting into trouble — legal trouble, that is.

"Let's save that argument for a different day," I smiled. "Right now, I have to get to work and figure out what's going on here."

She tapped my knee as she stood up to leave. "Just promise me you won't end up in the back of some creep's car this time."

"I will do my best," I gave her a reassuring smile.

"I love you, sweetie," she said as she left my room. "Please be careful."

"I will."

She left my room and I was left alone with my thoughts and my legal pad.

What did I already know?

I knew that whoever the killer was hated me and thought I was a killer.

I knew that they had murdered one person and attempted the murder of another in the exact same spot, using the exact same sentiments in two separate notes, which were placed somewhere on the person's body. Both notes were written with a red marker.

I knew that Mable owned the antique shop a few doors down and called me a murderer every chance she could get. She also had a small and miserly group of friends who also shared her opinions about me.

I knew that the *Coffee Creek Real Estate* office was located at the top of Main Street and there were two very busy agents trying to shift James Popper's paperwork over to ensure that his commissions were put in the right place, whatever that meant.

And Piper was an odd child. I didn't know if the weird stares I was getting from her meant anything. Perhaps, she was just a very introverted person who was afraid of anything, or anyone, she didn't know.

I finished jotting all of these things down on my notepad before flipping the page.

Who were Mable's friends?

I thought this might be as good a spot as any to start as Mable was the one who was actually calling me a murderer. Even though Mable wasn't strong enough to do the things that had happened, if she, somehow, had help from some, or all, of the women in her inner circle, the killing of James Popper might have just been a crime that they were capable of pulling off.

Plus, the timing would have been right.

James Popper was murdered before my mother, Reba and I had finished dinner on the night of the closing. I'd seen James earlier that day to sign the paperwork. Mable and her crew came into the restaurant as we were leaving.

Who was with her? There was Dotty Brennon, I remembered seeing her. I closed my eyes and tried to see the others in my mind. There were four ladies around Mable if I was correct. Wendy Ferris was also there. I was sure of it. And the last one would have been, Fern Rosewood.

It still seemed like a stretch, but it was possible that they somehow lured James onto the deck, had him sit down in a chair, and then ambushed him and strangled him with his own tie.

As I thought about what he must've gone through, how horrible the process of dying in that way must've been, my eyes welled with tears.

There was one thing I was having trouble figuring out. How would they have gotten into the building without the key? Had James had an extra key in his pocket? Had they convinced him to open the shop and give them a tour? Would James have done that for them after the closing had been finalized? Or, had they overpowered him and taken a key from him? Where had this occurred? If it occurred at all. Was there even a key to speak of? Clearly, there must've been an extra key. How else would they have gotten in there in the first place?

And if they used an extra key, that meant that the key was still out there.

Which made this investigation all the more important to wrap up quickly.

At this point, it looked like my first step was to go pay Dotty Brennon a visit.

She lived a few blocks from Main Street in a tiny yellow house with beautiful gardens, which she tended daily. She was fit as a fiddle, that one.

I looked at my phone.

It was a little after ten O'clock. If was going to be sweet as honey tomorrow, I was going to have to get some sleep.

Tomorrow, I would be wide awake and ready to catch a killer!

14

Dotty Brennon was spry for a woman in her seventies. She went for vigorous walks every day through town, could be seen with groups of friends up and down Main Street regularly, shopping and conversing. She also frequented many of the local restaurants and took care of all of her own yard work.

She owned a half acre corner lot a few blocks from Main Street. The house was quaint and yellow, with a beautiful little front porch on the front of it. The porch had two chairs, one for Dotty, and one that remained empty. It had been occupied by her husband, Harold, for fifty years before he passed a few years back.

As I drove my car up to her house, I slowed down and looked to see if she was outside. I didn't really feel like climbing up onto her porch and ringing the doorbell if I didn't have to.

I spotted her, in the middle of the yard, pulling a large bag of potting soil out of a tiny shed. Her hair, which looked like it had spent the night in large curlers, and whose pale yellow clearly came out of a bottle, was bouncing as she tugged the bag out into the yard.

She was such a small thing, and yet so strong. She took that bag of soil, which I guessed had to weigh at least twenty-five pounds, and threw it right over her shoulder.

Her walk wasn't inhibited by the sudden stress of the weight that she had just taken on. She walked quickly across the yard and threw the bag of soil down next to the foundation of the house.

I said a quick prayer and remembered my scripture from this morning's java and Jesus session. It was about courage, which I needed an abundance of at the moment.

> *Be strong and courageous. Do not be afraid or terri-*
> *fied because of them, for the LORD your God*
> *goes with you; he will never leave you nor*
> *forsake you."*
> *Deuteronomy 31:6-8*

With that in mind, I pulled my car into the driveway and killed the engine. I stepped out onto the hot blacktop.

It was sweltering, and just walking over to Dotty was

causing me to sweat. I couldn't imagine how she was doing all of this work out in the heat like she was.

My mother always reminded me that her generation and the generations before her were much tougher than my generation and the generations that were following us.

As I approached Dotty now, I most definitely agreed with my mother's assessment of things.

"Excuse me," I called out, once I thought I was within earshot. I didn't want to sneak up on her. She might accuse me of trying to murder her if I didn't let her know I was there before I got too close.

She had just picked the bag of soil up after cutting the top off with a rather large, sharp-looking knife, which she'd deposited in the grass next to her.

When she heard my voice, she looked around and set the bag of soil down with a thud. She picked up the knife and held it in front of herself, defensively.

"What do you want?" She asked me through squinted eyes.

"I just want to talk to you, Mrs. Brennon."

She held the knife forward a bit. "Well, go ahead. Talk."

"I realize this is very strange," I began. "But I saw you with Mable the other night. I already know what Mable thinks of me."

"You mean that you're a murderer?" Dotty interrupted.

"Yes," I nodded. "She thinks I'm a murderer. I'm actually here, not because *I'm* a murderer, but because I'm trying to figure out *who* the murderer is."

"Well, how am I supposed to help you with that?" Dotty shrugged. "I'm just taking care of my gardens, minding my own business."

"I understand that. I just wanted to talk to you about the other night."

"What about it?"

"James Popper was found dead just after I saw you with Mable and the others."

"So?"

I swallowed hard. "I was wondering what you were doing before you went to dinner with Mable?"

Her face changed slowly as she realized what I was asking.

She threw the knife, point first, into the yard and left it there, sticking straight out of the ground as she proceeded to charge me.

"You've got a lot of nerve coming over here, missy. I'll tell ya where I was!"

I began retreating to my car.

Dotty followed me all the way out to the driveway.

"I was with Mable at the antique shop. We, girls, meet up there. Mable always has a few bottles of wine chilling in a small fridge behind her counter. And we have a few glasses before we go to dinner because what the restaurants do to their wine prices is highway robbery. We refuse to pay for more than one glass! So, while James Popper was being strangled on *your* deck, the ladies and I were having a little pre-meal toddy…not that that's any of your business, nosy little thing that you are."

I had already hopped into my car and had the door closed with the window down when Dotty finished telling me how ridiculous my first theory was.

"I'm sorry I bothered you," I said. "But you do know that I was eating dinner while James Popper was murdered, right? Would you be willing to bring that information to Mable so she stops calling me a murderer every time I walk down the street?"

"I will do nothing of the sort," Dotty huffed. "Just because you were eating before we arrived at the restaurant doesn't make you innocent of James Popper's murder, any more than it makes you innocent of the murder of the poor golfer that died here back in May. Once a murderer, always a murderer." She made a motion with her hands like she was trying to get dust or sand off of them, clapping them up and down repeatedly. "I wash my hands of you, my poor misguided girl. Repentance for your sins is the only way to go through the narrow gate of the Lord."

I nodded. "I know that. I just wish you and Mable did."

I started my car and pulled out of her driveway, ignoring the outraged look on Dotty's face. I was headed for Wendy Ferris's. I didn't think I was going to make any headway with her, either, but it was worth a try.

WENDY FERRIS WAS nothing like Dotty Brennon, except for the fact that she thought I was a murderer and liked to spend her time with Mable.

She was frail and had the appearance of a skeleton draped with skin. Her gray hair was wavy and not given much attention. She had wide, round glasses with very thick lenses.

Her house was smack dab in the middle of a small housing development behind the *Coffee Creek Elementary School.* It was a drab gray with navy blue shutters and trim. There was no garden to speak of, not even so much as a shrub. Her grass was high and wispy with overgrown weeds.

I parked out in front and walked up a short and narrow sidewalk, my legs tickled by the weeds that were growing toward each other in an attempt to form an arch.

Before I even put my foot on the front steps, I heard Wendy's voice.

"You can stay right there!" She warned.

I stopped momentarily. The sun was situated behind the house and was sending its bright beams directly into my eyes, making it impossible to see Wendy.

"Ms. Ferris," I said, holding my hands up like I was

under arrest. "I promise, I'm not here to do anything other than talk."

I heard a loud click.

"What was that?"

"You come any closer and I will make you wish you listened better."

"Are you pointing a gun at me right now?" I asked. All of my scripture reading and focus on courage were starting to slowly walk away from me at that moment. And I was thinking, it might not be a bad idea to join them and live to fight another day.

"You're darn tootin' I'm pointing a gun at you! Do you think I'm just going to stand here unarmed when I have a known murderer walking up onto my property? Now, you get the heck out of here, or I'll be calling the cops to come to pick your dead body up off my sidewalk. This is my house and I have a right to defend it!"

I realized, at that moment, that, perhaps, Wendy Ferris wasn't going to give me anything to work with.

Backing away slowly, I kept my hands raised and said, "Wendy, I am going to leave now. I'm sorry I disturbed you. Please go back to whatever you were doing before I arrived and I will never bother you again."

"You just focus on getting yourself out of here and leave me to worry about what I'm going to do with the rest of my day."

I took a deep, shaky breath as I reached the driver's

seat of my car. Before I got in, Wendy had one more warning for me.

"Don't you dare go over to Fern's house, either! She has a bigger gun than I do."

I started the car and drove away as quickly as I could and I didn't stop until I was home.

15

D ear God,
Wow!
That's all I can say.

Alright, maybe that's not all I can say. But I will tell you that I am in a fair amount of shock here at what I just encountered.

I knew those women had hateful hearts, and that, dear Lord, is really between you and them, so I'm going to go ahead and get out of the conversation for that one.

But I was threatened at gunpoint and had a knife held up to me in the span of ten minutes by two women who look like they should be drinking tea and eating shortbread cookies in the air conditioning on a day like today.

What in the world was that?

I mean, holy cow…actually, I take that back. I know you're not too keen on the whole holy cow thing.

But you know what I mean, right?

Was that an overreaction on their part? Or is this an overreaction of mine?

Were you trying to send me a sign that I should not be interfering, or are you trying to tell me that those women who hang with Mable are capable of doing heinous things like strangling a real estate agent and shooting a police officer in the back?

Again, oh Lord, I am very confused by this whole thing. I'm beginning to feel like I am just going through this world in a perpetual state of confusion, from which there is no delivery.

Is that normal?

Does everyone else feel the way I do about these things?

I'll tell ya what I'm going to do. I'm going to call up Reba and go have some lunch with her. She might be able to offer some perspective about what's going on here.

Thanks for listening to me vent, God. I know this doesn't seem like it was a productive prayer, but for me, sometimes I just need to get things off my chest.

Right now, I'm thinking a burger and beer at the P&G with Reba might just put a little bit of perspective back into my life.

I'll pray with you later.

Thank you, and in your holy name, I pray.

AMEN

16

Reba was thrilled at the prospect of lunch at the *Pub & Grub*. I'd told her to meet me at the top of Main Street, on the corner near the *Coffee Creek Savings & Loan*.

"Why?" She asked. "You don't think there'll be parking down by the restaurant?"

"It's not that," I'd told her. "I just want to take a quick walk and see what else is going on."

"Mmmhmmm," she uttered, suspiciously. "That doesn't sound like a very full version of the truth if you ask me."

"Well, I'm not asking you. Meet me in front of the bank or you can pay for your own lunch."

That was all it took.

"You got it, boss. Whatever you say!"

Reba and her boyfriend Dillon were in a state of constant saving. They had good reason, as they wanted to get out of their apartment and into a house, plus a wedding seemed inevitable. Reba had grown up relatively poor, so she knew her parents weren't going to be much help on the financial support side of things where that was concerned. And according to Reba, Dillon's parents were a bit on the traditional side and expected the bride's parents to foot the bill for a wedding if it were ever to happen.

They weren't totally sold on the idea that Reba and Dillon were going to last in the first place. Thankfully, Dillon was willing to add a fair amount of his own money to the wedding fund they had going. In return, he expected Reba to pinch her pennies, too, and not spend their money frivolously.

I didn't mind throwing the occasional twenty dollars Reba's way. She was a good egg, and a lot of fun to be around. And I knew that someday if I could ever get out of this blasted murder cloud I was under, she would be the premier barista at Connie's Cafe. Her ability to make great coffee when given high-end ingredients, as well as her stunning good looks and fun-loving charm, made her a no-brainer to hire as the face of the coffee counter.

She arrived just a few seconds after I did, pulling her car over and parking on the opposite side of the road, directly across from my car.

Her purple locks were hanging loose down her face.

She gave me a sultry look through her opened window, winking and blowing me a kiss.

"You're something else," I said, laughing while I got out of my car. "What are we going to do with you?"

"I think you should take me to lunch," she said, crossing the road and putting her hair up in a high, tight ponytail.

"It's on the docket," I grinned.

We got onto the sidewalk and turned right at the corner past the bank and started our walk toward the *P&G*.

Behind the bank was *Coffee Creek Real Estate*. I noticed there was a closed sign in their doorway.

"That's interesting," I said, pointing to the note in the doorway. "You would think that with two people in the office, one of them would be able to stay there to cover things."

Reba shrugged. "What are ya gonna do about it?"

"Nothing," I said, "it just seems strange to me, that's all."

"Like poop paper?" She smiled. "People do things in different ways, ya know."

"Yeah," I said, "I guess."

We were about a hundred feet away from Mable's shop and I could feel my body tighten up. I had chosen this walk to lunch intentionally, with the idea that Mable would come out and start yelling at me again.

But as I got closer to it, I suddenly didn't want it anymore.

Much to my surprise, she did not come out.

As we walked by her shop, I turned my head and tried to get a view of what was going on inside.

Also, much to my surprise, I saw that Mable was not alone inside. She had a guest with bright pink hair and piercings galore.

"What's Piper doing in there?" I mused.

"Who's Piper?" Reba asked.

"Nothing," I said, continuing to watch the interaction. I stopped walking completely.

"Come on, Connie," Reba encouraged. "Let's go. I only have an hour before I have to be back to work."

"Just a moment," I said. "You'll get back on time."

Mable and Piper were having what looked to be a very pleasant conversation. If one didn't know any better, one could've guessed that they were very good friends. At one point, Piper actually smiled.

"Connie?" Reba tapped her foot on the sidewalk. "How long are you going to stand here looking like a creeper?"

"As long as I need to," I said. "If you want to go get us a table, I'll be there in a minute."

Reba huffed. "No, I'll wait."

I'm glad she did. Because the next thing I knew, Mable was handing Piper some folded-up bills, which Piper slid into her pocket. Then Mable gave her a package of red permanent markers.

She said something to Piper, and the girl nodded.

As Piper was walking to the door, Mable saw me watching and walked out of her shop onto the sidewalk.

I tapped Reba on the back. "Time to go."

"It's about time," Reba grumbled.

We began moving toward the *P&G*, but the damage had been done.

"Murderer!" Mable yelled behind us, as Piper ran past us toward *Reads & Teas*.

Rebecca was standing out front, her hand held out in a questioning way. "Where have you been?" She asked Piper as the girl ran into the shop.

Rebecca looked up at me and shook her head.

"Snoop!" Mable blurted out. "She's a murderer and a snoop, that one!"

Reba and I finally turned onto the flower-lined sidewalk that led up to the *Pub & Grub*. We could not get inside fast enough.

"I don't know what that was," Reba said, catching her breath. "But your life is way more exciting than mine."

"You don't even know the half of it."

PENNY SIMPSON WAS at her usual post.

"Two, outside?" She asked us as we approached the

front of the restaurant.

I looked at Reba and said, "Do you mind if we sit inside today?"

"Not at all," Reba smiled.

"We'll be inside," I said, turning to Penny. "Thanks."

She took us through the bar area and I saw why the *Coffee Creek Real Estate* office was closed.

Both, Tiffany Elizabeth and Matthew Grant were sitting at the bar. *They were sitting remarkably close for colleagues,* I thought to myself. Matthew was sitting on a high back chair, his legs spread out and his feet resting on the chair next to him. Tiffany was on that chair, her legs were tucked inside of his with her feet resting on the bottom of his chair.

She kept touching his legs as she drank what appeared to be a margarita. He was sipping on a light beer.

As we walked by, they raised their drinks in a quiet toast. I overheard Matthew say, "To the smartest, most successful realtors in Coffee Creek." They clinked glasses and took a healthy drink off of their beverages.

Penny guided us to a small table in the corner of the dining room. It was near the painting of a boat at sea with a massive wave in front of it. I'd seen this painting many times and yet it still held so much power as I sat down and stared at it again. It reminded me of faith in times of peril.

"The best of both worlds," Penny smiled. "You've got a seat inside." She turned and pointed to the giant French doors, "But you've also got a great view of the creek!"

"Thank you very much," I said.

Penny nodded and placed our menus in front of us. "I'll give you ladies a few minutes to look things over, okay?"

"So, how's it going?" Reba asked after Penny walked away.

"I don't know," I said, trying not to be too frumpy. "Things are really weird, that's all."

"Tell me about it," she nodded. "This morning I was pouring coffee and taking orders, and Gerry actually came out to help."

Gerry had been my boss at the coffee shop we do not name. It would've taken an earthquake or a fire to get him out of his office during his shift most days.

"Really?" I smirked. "Bet that caught you by surprise."

"A little. But I wasn't *that* surprised. He caught wind that you bought the place on Main Street, and he may have heard from someone that you were planning on hiring me."

"And who would he have heard that from?"

"I dunno," she grinned. "A little birdy might've told him."

"So, you think he's trying to get you to stay by being a little extra helpful?"

"Possibly."

"Is it going to work?" I asked. "Do I need to start looking for another all-star barista?"

"Of course, it's not going to work." She flashed a sly

grin, "But what Gerry doesn't know, won't hurt him. Plus, during that morning rush, I'll take all the help I can get!"

I nodded. "I know what you mean."

"You said it's been weird for you, too?"

"Yeah, a little," I answered. I didn't know how much I really wanted to get into things with Reba. For one, it had been a few days since I'd seen her and she'd made it clear that she didn't want to get involved in everything. For two, we were in public and the *P&G*, though not filled to capacity, was in the middle of a moderately busy lunch hour.

"What do you mean, a little?" Reba pressed. "Are you any closer to catching the killer? You know, I heard a cop was shot in your shop yesterday. Is that true?"

"Could you keep it down a little?" I shot her a less-than-pleasant look. "This is fairly sensitive information."

"Right," she said, cringing at her own stupidity. "Sorry."

"It's okay," I whispered. I leaned forward, and so did Reba. "Yes, it's true that Officer Freeman was shot in the same spot where you discovered James Popper."

"Oh my goodness," she said, her eyes widening. "Is he…"

"No, he's not dead. He'll be alright," I said. "Thank God for big favors."

"No kidding," she nodded.

"I went to visit a few of Mable's friends this morning."

"You did not!" She put her hand on mine. "Girl, you'd

better be careful. That's a rough-looking crew she was with the other night. You'd better watch your six or you're going to end up next on the *murdered in Coffee Creek list.*"

"*Watch your six?* Is that even a thing?" I chuckled at her.

"I saw it in a movie once…shut up."

"Also, this list that you speak of, I'm doing my best to stay off that one. But you, being my friend, are a prime candidate, I'm afraid."

I smiled. Reba didn't.

"You're a real jerk," she said, sitting back, and taking her hand off of mine. "Now, I'm not going to sleep for a month because I'm going to be afraid that someone's out to get me."

"Sorry," I laughed. "I was just joking. I couldn't help myself."

"Yeah, well, maybe you work on that self-control thing you're always preaching about."

To be fair, I think I'd brought up self-control once or twice with Reba over the few years we'd known each other. But she'd been so flummoxed by the mention of it, that she'd really internalized the lesson and had convinced herself that it was one of the things I always talked about.

"I don't always preach about it," I giggled, "but you do bring up a good point. I should have thought a little bit more before I made that joke."

"Anyway, you went to see Mable's friends this morning. What happened? Obviously, you're still alive, so it couldn't have been that bad."

"You'd be surprised." I raised my eyebrows. "I had a knife pulled on me by Dotty Brennon, and was practically chased off her property. She's a real pitbull, you know. Now, to be fair to her, she did throw the knife into the ground before she chased me back to my car."

"Like, *by your feet* into the ground," Reba asked.

"No, like *straight* down. She wasn't trying to hurt me or anything like that. I think she just wanted me to know that she was not a person I should reckon with."

Reba nodded. "Sounds like she sent that message loud and clear."

"Amen to that, sister." I took a sip of the water that was on the table when we'd sat down. "After that, I went to see Wendy Ferris."

"Oh," Reba rolled her eyes. "She's a bird, isn't she?"

"I don't know," I shrugged. "I didn't get close enough to her to find out."

"What are you talking about?"

"I was halfway up her sidewalk when she pulled a gun on me."

"What kind of gun?"

"I don't know. The sun was in my eyes. But at that range, I don't think it would have mattered that much what kind of gun she had, I'd have been a goner for sure."

"No, you knucklehead," Reba shook her head. "You just said Officer Freeman was shot twice in the back, didn't you?"

"I did."

"Do you think it's possible that those old bats attacked him at your place and that Wendy Ferris pulled the trigger?"

The thought sent the hairs on the back of my neck standing up. At this point, anything was possible.

"I guess, I should give Ted a call and see what he thinks."

"Ted?" Reba asked, giving me a puzzled look.

"Oh, wow," I said, shaking my head. "A lot has happened in the last few days, I suppose. Officer Billings and I are kind of on a first-name basis now." I blushed.

"Oh, really?"

"Yeah."

"How did that happen? Did your mother ask him out for you?"

"How did you know?" I asked, blushing an even deeper shade of red than before.

"Shut up!" She laughed. "I was joking about that. Your mother really asked him out for you?"

"Yes," I nodded in shame. "She really did."

"How'd she do it? Did she make a bunch of cookies for you to bring over to the police station or something?"

"How did you know?"

"I may have told her that would work." Reba grinned, leaning back and folding her arms, very satisfied with herself.

17

After lunch, I headed home and went up to my bedroom to make some more notes on my yellow legal pad.

I wrote down Dotty's name first. Next to her name, I put a big question mark. I still didn't know what she was capable of if anything. She seemed angry, and she was definitely strong, but she put the knife down pretty quickly, and she mentioned the Lord. Anyone who mentions the Lord wouldn't kill someone to prove that murder was wrong, would they?

The next name I wrote down was Wendy Ferris. She had not mentioned God and had actually pulled a gun on me. Reba brought up a good point that her gun may have been the gun that shot Officer Freeman. I would have to check with Ted to see if they had uncovered any information in that regard. My guess was he wouldn't tell me. But maybe this newfound connection we had would result in me getting some inside intel.

Even though Wendy had a gun, it certainly didn't seem like she was capable of doing anything to James Popper without significant help. Plus, James wasn't shot. He was strangled, which would have taken a significant amount of strength.

That led me back to Dotty. But again, the God thing. I shook my head, trying to wrestle with everything. How could this be so darned difficult?

Next on the list was Mable. She hated my guts like no other person I'd ever encountered. Dotty had said that they were drinking before they went to dinner.

Could it have been possible that Mable and the girls got a little tipsy and murdered James on a whim?

And what was up with Piper getting paid by Mable and given a red marker like the one that was used to write the notes? They even used a combination of Mable's message of 'murderer' and Dotty's faith-based condemnation.

It was all so strange. The only one on the list of Mable's friends I hadn't seen was Fern Rosewood. She didn't strike me as being a terrifying figure. She was diminutive in stature and legally blind. At least, I thought that was what I'd heard about her.

So, was it possible that all four of Mable's friends had convinced James to let them into the building to look around? Then, once they had him out on the deck, they overpowered him, tied him to the chair, and choked him with his tie. And before they left, Mable stashed a note that Piper had written into the pocket of his shirt for the officers to find when they were investigating.

It didn't seem likely.

Was it possible?

Yes, it probably was possible.

But not probable.

I had to call Ted.

He answered after just one ring. *What a sweetie.*

"Hey Connie, how are you doing?"

"I'm doing well," I said. "Listen, not to be rude, but I really need the answer to a quick question, and then I have to get back to work."

"Okay?" His voice sounded suspicious, which I fully understood.

"Did James Popper have a key to my shop on his person at the time of his murder?"

"What are you doing, Connie?"

"Nothing," I said. "Can you please just answer the question?"

"You know I can't do that."

"Are you sure?" I started to turn up the charm with my sweet and innocent voice. "Not even for me?"

"Especially not for you," he said. "If anything ever happened to you, I wouldn't be able to live with myself."

"That's so kind of you to say," I replied. "Can you hear me blushing through the phone?"

"What?"

"Never mind," I said, trying to move on from my failed attempt at humor. "Are you sure you can't give me just one little crumb?"

He sighed deeply.

"I'll tell you what," he said. "Hang up and I'll text you a one-letter response."

"Thanks," I said. "I owe you."

"Goodbye, Connie."

He hung up and I waited for his text.

It never came.

I WAS FUMING! How dare he tell me that he was going to help me out and then just hang up on me without doing what he promised?

Fine.

I'd have to solve this without him.

The key. That was everything as far I was concerned. If James had it on his person when he went into the shop, then it was possible that Mable and her crew committed the crime.

Of course, It was possible that they took the key with them after the murder took place.

And if that happened, that meant that a murderer

now had possession of the key to my shop. That was a scary thought.

Who else, besides James could have had the key to the shop?

Would they have kept an extra key at the realtor's office? If they did, then it was possible that Matthew Grant and Tiffany Elizabeth had it.

That made me feel a little better.

That was until I really started to turn it over in my mind. Could they have killed James?

Of course, they could have.

The real question was, did they?

What would their motive be?

Mable's motive seemed clear — to send me a message that she wasn't going to tolerate someone that she deemed a murderer establishing a business on her street. That I could kind of understand.

But why would James Popper's colleagues kill him? Were they jealous of him? He did have a reputation for being the best realtor in Coffee Creek. Was that it?

That seemed like a pretty weak motive. There had to be more.

I had to take a break. All this thinking was making me hungry.

MOTHER DIDN'T DISAPPOINT.

She had made us homemade veggie pizza with a nice semi-dry Riesling. The two went together perfectly and helped to pick me up a bit.

"Hey," she said, about halfway through dinner, "I have a question."

"What's that?"

"Do you have any idea why Teddy would be sending me a text?"

"He sent you a text?" I was flabbergasted. He wouldn't even send me the text that he promised me, and here he was firing off messages to my mother.

"Yes," she said, squinting at her screen as she typed in her password and retrieved the message in question. "He sent it at three thirty, and it says only one letter: *N*."

"Is that it?" I laughed as I stood up to get another slice of pizza and another glass of wine.

"Yes," she said, scrolling through all of her messages.

"Mom," I chuckled, "Your phone doesn't work like that. If he sent you more, it would have been there with the first one."

"Oh," she said, "okay." She put her phone away. "Well, in that case, that's all he sent."

I smirked.

"Do you know what that means?" She asked, crinkling up her nose.

"As a matter of fact, I do."

"Well, are you going to tell me, or not?"

I smiled. "It means Ted knows how to use his phone about as well as you know how to use yours."

"Smart aleck," my mother slapped me.

"I do have one question. How does Ted have your number?"

"Well, dear, sometimes your mother needs to set things up with others without you knowing."

"Are you serious?" I asked, my mouth hanging in disbelief. "Reba said the cookies were her idea. Are you telling me that Ted knew we were coming to the station beforehand?"

She shrugged, smirking her way through a sip of wine. "Maybe."

"You guys are unbelievable," I exclaimed, sitting back in my chair. "I'm going to have a talk with Ted about having conversations with you behind my back."

My mother just shrugged.

18

Ted came by after dinner. My mother, thankfully, stayed inside and cleaned up the kitchen before retiring to the living room for a Hallmark movie.

It was one I hadn't seen, and I would have loved to have watched it with her. But I wasn't about turning down an evening with Ted, either.

"What do you want to do?" He asked as he joined me in a chair on the front porch.

"I don't know," I shrugged. "If you don't mind, I'd just kind of like to sit here and talk."

"Whew," he said, swiping his hand across his forehead dramatically. "I was hoping you'd say that. Today was a busy day, and the thought of going out and doing something late into the night, was more than I was really hoping for. Sitting here with you, though. I'm up for that."

I smiled at him.

"While I've got you in a good mood," I began, "can we talk about you and my mother texting each other?"

He stood up and walked away from me. "Well, it was a lot of fun getting to know you. You're a real swell gal," he joked.

"Get over here and sit down, goofy," I laughed, pointing at his chair. "But I'm serious. You can't send my mother messages behind my back and expect me to trust you."

He nodded. "I understand. That was an honest mistake, though. I really did mean to text you, I just hit the wrong Cafe in my contacts list."

"I get that," I said. "But I'm not just talking about this time. I mean all the time. And granted, it's not lost on me that we're spending this wonderful time together because you and my mother and Reba went behind my back. But now that we're here, you can just communicate with me, okay?"

"Okay," He smiled. "I will just text or call you. Scout's honor."

"Can we talk about something else?"

"That depends." He sat up straight and turned to face me. "You know there are things I'm not allowed to talk to you about. Things like the James Popper case."

"Am I that obvious?"

"Yeah. You are," he chuckled, shaking his head and staring off into the distance.

"I just can't tell you how devastating it is to have someone murdered because they helped you. You don't know what that's like."

"You're right," he said. "I don't. But you can't understand how hard it is to want to keep that person safe when she goes all over town looking for a lead and ends up with a gun pointed at her face."

"You heard about that?"

"Yeah," he nodded. "I heard."

"How?"

"One of Ms. Ferris's neighbors called it in. Turns out she points that thing at just about anyone who comes to her door, especially if she doesn't know them. Between you and me, she's starting to lose it up here, a little." He pointed to the side of his head. "Anyway, that's not the point. The point is, you don't know what you're doing, and if you keep it up, one of these days, the gun's not just going to be pointed, it's going to get fired. And that, Connie, is just a little more than I'm prepared to handle at this point in time."

I nodded, remorsefully. "I know. I understand. It's just...have you ever had a compulsion. Something within you that you just can't seem to control? That's the way I feel about finding whoever did this."

He nodded and smiled. "Why do you think I became a cop? I've always had the compulsion to stop the bad guys. When I was a kid I was *obsessed* with superheroes…with a capital *O*. At about the age of twelve, I started to realize there were no such things as superheroes. Not the ones I was used to anyway. There were no masked men in capes and tight underwear, flying around and saving the innocent people of the city from certain doom. But, there were professions, like police officers who tried to fill that role, all be it without the tight underwear — on the outside of their uniform, that is."

We both laughed. It felt good. Sitting here with Ted made me realize how good I had it to have a guy like him on my side. He was so many things that I'd been missing.

"But seriously," he said, finishing up his laugh, and bringing his voice down. "Please, don't go down to Main Street tomorrow. Please, don't drive all over the place searching for clues, or the next lead, or eyewitness testimony. Can you please just stay home for the day, watch some TV, read some books, play a board game with your mother, or whatever else you do, and then be ready for me at seven O'clock when I pick you up for dinner?"

"I think I can manage that," I nodded.

He stood up.

"Okay, then. It's settled. I'll take you to dinner tomorrow night. Right now, I'm going to head home. I am pretty wiped out."

"Sounds, good," I said, standing up and walking him

to the end of the porch. "Get some rest and I'll see you tomorrow."

As he drove off, I couldn't pull myself away from the porch, even after his taillights were long out of view. There was something happening to me. And I had an idea that I knew what it was.

19

The next morning I was awoken by the buzzing of my phone on the nightstand next to my bed. *What time was it?*

I picked up my phone and saw that I was getting a call from Ted.

That's odd. He would never call me at this hour, would he?

"Hello," I said into the phone, trying not to sound too much like I was still asleep.

"Hey, Connie," Ted's voice came through. It wasn't soothing and calm like usual. Rather, it was tentative and shaky, like he had some more unpleasant news for me. "Did I wake you?"

"Don't worry about it," I said, sitting up. "What's up?"

"I wanted you to hear this from me before you heard it from anyone else."

"Okay…"

"We've arrested a teenager by the name of Piper Lomback."

My heart jumped into my throat. What had Piper been arrested for? Was she being accused of the murder of James Popper? Did this have something to do with the money she had gotten from Mable the day before? Could she have been the one who shot Officer Freeman in the back?

I thought about Rebecca who'd given her niece an opportunity and gotten paid back in the most ungrateful way possible. Poor Rebecca.

"What did she do?" I asked.

"She was caught this morning posting nasty messages on all of the storefronts. They were all written in red maker like the notes we found on James Popper and Officer Freeman. Every one of them alludes to you being a murderer and you suffering some form of eternal damnation."

"That's awful," I said, struggling to find words to comment on the shock of everything I'd just been told.

"We think she has a connection to the murderer," Ted told me. "Detective Tolbert is going to interview her later."

"Okay," I swallowed hard. "What does that mean for me?"

"It means that you should do exactly what we talked

about last night. Stay home, and lay low. And I'm going to be sending Donald West over to your house to make sure you and your mother aren't in any imminent danger."

"Didn't Detective Tolbert tell you not to do that?"

"That was before these messages got posted all over town. As things change, we have to change. We believe that there is now a definite risk to your safety. Don't worry, Officer West will stay outside, in your driveway, just to make sure that nobody tries to do anything to you at your house."

"Thank you, Ted. What am I supposed to tell my mother?"

"Don't worry about that," he said. "I have her in my contacts. I'll give her a call and fill her in on the situation. You just sit tight until I pick you up for dinner tonight."

"We're still going to dinner?"

"Oh yeah," Ted said, his voice finally playful and fun. "Nobody's going to mess with you, out in public, with me. Plus, I've got Officer Snelling set up for the night shift at your house. Just in case you were worried about your mother."

"Thanks, Ted. I owe you." I said.

"Just promise me you'll wait."

"Cross my heart, hope *not* to die."

I thought that was pretty funny.

Ted did not.

WHEN I FINALLY MADE MY way downstairs, my mother was at her usual spot in the corner of the kitchen, waiting for the coffee maker to do its thing.

She was still in her fluffy yellow bathrobe, tapping her slippered foot on the floor. Her red hair was wild.

"Good morning," she said. Her voice was steady and her mouth was straight, not an ounce of cheer to be found.

"Good morning," I returned, heading to the cupboard to get my big mug.

"I've already got it," my mother held it up. "I've got the other one too," she winked, holding up the matching mug that, most days, went unused.

"Are you okay?" I asked her.

She sighed. "I suppose so. I'm about as okay as any woman can be when she finds out that her daughter might be the target of a deranged killer."

"That might be a little dramatic." I smiled, trying to break the tension.

My mother snapped.

"Connie, they're sending an armed officer to our house for round-the-clock protection. Do you really think I'm being dramatic? We aren't allowed to leave the house until they find out who's doing these things. Do you really think I'm being dramatic?"

The coffee maker did its end of percolation gurgle, followed by a deep sigh of relief at a job well done. My mother poured our mugs full to the brim and handed me mine.

We sat down at the kitchen table, sipping our coffee and staring off into space, neither one of us saying a word to the other.

I wanted to tell my mother that I was sorry. But the more I thought about it, the more I realized I didn't have anything to be sorry about. I was just living my life. I'd been accused of murder by *The Gazette* after David Gardner's murder. I hadn't murdered anyone. I'd been set up. And most people knew it. But someone was trying to make it look like these people were dying because of me somehow. That just wasn't true.

It made me so angry to think that my life, my mother's life, the police department, the people of Coffee Creek, James Popper, and Officer Freeman could all be so affected by the perpetuation of the lies of Jeff Toobin and Sheila Robinson.

But what could I do about it?

The damage had been done, and the only thing that I was able to do was to sit inside my house and lay low until the authorities got things under control.

"So are you going out tonight with Ted?" My mother finally asked.

"Yes," I nodded.

"I think that's a good idea. He'll be there to protect you. And they're going to send someone over to watch over me too."

"Hopefully, they can figure out something before dinner tonight," I said, optimistically.

"Time will tell, my dear," my mother said. "Time will tell."

20

A s it turned out, time did tell.

Actually, the time came and went and nothing happened.

My mother and I spent the day watching Hallmark movies, drinking coffee, and spending time on our own, in our rooms diving into books and scripture.

Every minute that went by seemed like an hour, and every hour that went by seemed like an eternity.

I finally got around to taking a shower around six O'clock in the evening, and the only reason I was that ambitious was that Ted was coming to pick me up for dinner at seven.

He arrived on time with a serious look on his face. He was dressed in a nice pair of navy blue pants, and a sky blue polo. He smelled of mint gum and fancy cologne.

"Are you okay?" I asked.

"I'm better now," he said, flashing a quick smile to put me at ease.

"How are things going? You know, finding the murderer?"

"I can't really tell you," he said. "But I can say that it's been slow going. Much slower than we were hoping for."

"So, should we just stay in tonight?" I asked, thinking that I didn't care what we did, I just really wanted to be around him.

"No," he said. "We'll go have a proper date. It'll be good to help get my mind off of things."

"My mother…"

"She'll be fine. I've actually got two officers outside the house right now. One in the driveway, keeping an eye on the front of the house, and the other is in the back, making sure that nobody tries to sneak onto the property using an alternative route."

I nodded and gave him a hug. "Thank you."

He hugged me back.

My mother came down the stairs. She was still in her fluffy yellow bathrobe, her hair even less tame than before, which I didn't think was possible.

"I didn't have anywhere to go tonight," she smiled at Ted. "I hope you don't mind that I didn't get dressed up for the occasion."

"No, ma'am. You look perfect just the way you are."

He smiled and filled her in on the security situation for the evening.

"Very well," my mother nodded. "I assume you will be taking precautions to protect my daughter this evening, as well."

"Absolutely, Mrs. Cafe. She will be safer than safe, no doubt about it."

My mother nodded and gave me a kiss on the cheek.

"Well, in that case, have fun."

Ted had gotten us a reservation at the *Coffee Creek Surf & Turf*.

I shot him a glance when we pulled up to the restaurant.

"Is there something wrong?" He asked as he turned the truck off.

"This is the place we had dinner the night James Popper was murdered."

"Sorry," he said. "I didn't know. I figured I wanted to take you out to the nicest restaurant around. I didn't mean to bring up bad memories for you. I can cancel the reservation if you'd like."

I could hear the disappointment in his voice as the idea of canceling the reservation was spoken.

"No," I shook my head. "It's okay. This is sweet, what you've done. Let's go try to have a nice time."

"Are you sure?"

"Yes," I nodded. "I'm positive."

We walked up the steps and into the front of the restaurant. It was quiet as most of the dinner rush had already left. At seven thirty, we had our pick of seating.

Ted asked if we could sit out on the deck.

The deck had a spectacular view of the water, looking over Main Street and past the Gazebo and boat launch. From here, I could see *Reads and Teas*, the lights still on. I could make out Rebecca working both the tea counter and checking people out at the register.

Next to *Reads and Teas*, I could see my building. The windows were dark and the front of the place was wrapped with crime scene tape.

I felt tears welling up in my eyes at the idea of what might never become. Taking a deep breath, I held them back and quickly wiped my eyes before Ted could see me.

We took our seats and ordered drinks. Both of us ordered water.

"I've been looking forward to seeing you all day," Ted said, eyeing me past the menu.

"Me too," I said.

"What are you going to have?" He asked. "I, personally, love the chicken tenders and French fries."

I giggled, at first. Then, unable to contain myself, I burst out in a fit of laughter.

"Are you serious?" I asked him. "You come to a place like this for chicken tenders?"

"No," he shook his head, laughing just as hard as I was. "I just wanted to see what your reaction would be."

"That's too much," I said. "*Chicken tenders!*"

"Actually, I am a huge fan of the steamed mussels that they make, with the garlic and sauvignon blanc reduction."

I raised my eyebrow. "Ted Billings, I had no idea you were such a foodie."

He shrugged and smirked. "What can I say?"

"I also love a dish with the sauvignon blanc reduction. But it's not the mussels. Don't get me wrong, they taste great. But they can be a lot of work to eat. I prefer the pan-seared scallops with that same reduction. It is just perfection."

He nodded. "Perhaps, I'll try that tonight. I've never had it before."

"Well, you're in for a real treat."

At that moment, I caught something out of the corner of my eyes that took my attention away from my lovely conversation with Ted, which was no easy feat.

Matthew Grant and Tiffany Elizabeth were walking down Main Street together, holding hands. They stopped in front of my building and looked around. Then, as if they thought the coast was clear, they ducked under the police tape, pulled out a key, and went inside.

"Did you see that?" I asked.

"See what?" Ted asked.

"I'll be right back," I said, standing up and walking back inside the restaurant.

Ted didn't follow as he probably thought I was just using the bathroom.

I walked out onto Main Street and in the direction of Matthew and Tiffany.

As I approached the police tape, I heard Ted call my name from the deck of the restaurant.

"Connie! What are you doing?"

I ignored him and went inside.

I was going to find out what was going on once and for all.

21

I walked into the shop as quietly as I could. It was getting dark and difficult to see. Straining my ears, I listened, wondering where Matthew and Tiffany were.

After a moment, it became clear that they were not in the front end. I quietly walked behind the counter and into the kitchen. They weren't there, either.

That left the deck.

By the time I walked back out into the main area of the shop, Ted was already walking across the street and was on his way.

I went out onto the deck. Matthew and Tiffany were standing at the railing, embracing each other as the sun was dipping below the tree line of the creek.

"What are you doing here?" I spoke up.

They jumped, startled at the sudden realization that they were no longer alone.

"What are you doing here?" Tiffany asked. "Don't you know this place is a crime scene?"

Matthew laughed and then pulled out a gun and smiled. He pointed it at me and said, "And it's about to become one again."

"What are you doing?" I asked, shocked. "Why would you?"

"Well," Matthew said, "I wasn't going to tell you anything, but since you're going to be dead in a moment, you should at least know why."

"Shut up, Matt," Tiffany said. "Just shoot her and let's get out of here."

"You killed James Popper," I said. "And you shot Officer Freeman, too."

"Wow," Matthew smiled, "you are quite the sleuth, aren't you? Yes, it was Matthew Grant, on the deck, with the tie. And what a God-awful tie at that. You know, there was part of me that took great pleasure in killing him with that thing."

"You're sick," I snarled. "You shot Officer Freeman too?"

"Actually," Matthew nodded in Tiffany's direction. "That was her."

Tiffany shook her head and glared at Matthew. "What are you doing?"

"Just having a little bit of fun, babe."

"So, why did you kill James? Were you jealous of his reputation as the best realtor in Coffee Creek?"

"No," Matthew shook his head. "It wasn't jealousy."

"Then what was it? Money?"

"Mostly," Matthew nodded and looked at Tiffany. "Wouldn't you say that was most of it? I mean, it certainly wasn't the only reason. Some of that was his own fault. He was a little too nosy for his own good."

"Matthew, stop!" Tiffany demanded.

"I think I get it," I said, stepping forward.

"Stay where you are!" Matthew ordered.

"Why?" I asked. "You're going to shoot me anyway."

I felt like I could be a little brazen about things because Ted would be coming through that door at some point. I was just hoping that he would do it sooner than later.

"I'll tell ya what," Matthew smiled. "You go ahead and float your theory and if you're correct you'll get to live for a few minutes longer."

I took a deep breath.

Here goes nothing.

"I think you and Tiffany had an office romance that your boss didn't know about. James caught wind of it and threatened to blow you in. He also sold the biggest building on Main Street to a woman who was being harassed for being a suspected murderer. By killing him in this building, you could raise suspicion that either I, or Mable and her group of curmudgeonly friends, killed

James. You didn't write the note, but you found it taped to my door, and you thought that it would lead the cops to someone else. In the meantime, you took a few days to falsify the records of James's sales, giving you two all the credit for the sales, hence, you would get the commissions."

Matthew nodded. "You're very good at this."

"Thanks," I said.

Where was Ted?

"Officer Freeman was never supposed to get shot, but you were in here at the time, and you panicked when he came in to check on things. And I'm the last part of your plan. I don't think you wanted to kill me at first. You were just going to try to convince me to sell the building and give up the business, which would have given you a double commission. However, the police arrested the person who wrote the notes this morning, making the harassment seem far more innocent. But, if you kill me and get away with it, then you could convince my mother to sell the building."

"Bravo!" Matthew laughed.

And then he stopped and pointed the gun at me once again.

I closed my eyes and began praying to God, fully prepared to die.

Then I heard two shots ring loudly through the night.

22

"Connie?"

I heard a voice calling out to me from somewhere, but I couldn't locate it. There was darkness all around; darkness from which I couldn't pull myself free.

"Connie! Oh, God, Connie. Come on, wake up. Wake up, Connie!"

My eyes began to flutter. It was still impossible to make out what was happening around me in the darkness. There were loud noises.

A man screaming.

A woman shouted, "I didn't do anything! He's the killer!"

"Can you hear me?" I heard a voice to my left, and then I felt myself rise as if I was floating away on a cloud.

And I started to move backward.

A searing pain burned in my leg.

What is that?

"Connie? Can you hear me?"

That voice sounded familiar. It was moving with me, following me through the night.

I was weak. Too weak to open my eyes.

The man's screams and the woman's shouts fell away as I continued to move backward.

I took a deep breath, and then everything went black again.

23

Dear God,

You are good. I know this to be true with all of my being. And if this is the end, oh Lord, I am blessed to be joining you in Heaven. And I am blessed to have had the life that I have had, even if it wasn't what I'd hoped it was going to be.

This might sound a little funny, Lord, but I have visions of my father and me reuniting in heaven and opening up Connie's Cafe.

Do you think that would be possible?

You know my father better than I do. Do you think he would want to do something like that with me?

And could we save a spot for my mother at your table, oh Lord? I'm so sorry that I've put her through so much over the years.

She's a good woman.

And she would want nothing more than to meet up with my father one more time, for eternity this time.

I know this to be true, and so do you, dear God. So do you dear God.

If this is where my road on earth ends and my journey to your narrow gate begins, please take me in with open arms, for I am your humble servant.

Thank you for my life and all of the people you've put into it. Thank you for the experiences you've given me, both the good and the bad, for they are all good, or help in the search for good along the way.

I am forever indebted to you, Lord my God, redeemer, and defender of everything that I am and everything that I am to be.

In your holy name, I pray,

AMEN

24

I awoke in a room with dim fluorescent lights and beeps and murmurs.

There was tape on my hand and tubes coming out of my body. I followed them with my eyes to see where they led.

I was tired. Too tired to breathe, it seemed.

My mother was sitting in a chair next to my bed, and Ted was by her side, holding her hand.

They both rose when they saw that I was awake.

"Honey," my mother said, standing up and tapping Ted on the leg. "She's awake," she turned to tell him.

He stood up and rushed to the opposite side of the bed.

"Are you alright?" My mother asked. She was still in her fluffy yellow bathrobe and her hair was as wild as ever.

I nodded.

"Oh, thank heavens," she said, putting her hands together in front of her face. "Thank you, Jesus!"

I smiled faintly. I was thinking the same thing.

"Connie," Ted said, leaning forward, bringing his mouth close to my ear. I could smell his mint gum and cologne. Even after everything we'd been through, those smells survived. "Matthew and Tiffany were arrested, and thanks to your detective work, they'll be put away for a long time."

The memory of what had happened came rushing back to me. How, Ted had barged through the door at the last minute, and shot Matthew in the shoulder, forcing him to fall forward and fire a bullet into my leg. He'd lost control of the gun and I'd fallen backward. The last thing I remembered was Ted kicking the gun out of Matthew's reach and putting handcuffs on him before he grabbed Tiffany and held her back. Then I'd lost consciousness.

"You were late," I said.

Ted put his head down and wiped the tears from his eyes. "I know, Connie. I was. I should have been there sooner."

"I shouldn't have gone in there without you," I smiled. "That was pretty dumb, huh?"

"That's one way to describe it," my mother rolled her eyes. "The good Lord was on our side tonight, thank God."

"I'm sorry," I said to both of them. "I never should have rushed in after them."

"Well, thankfully things worked out the way they did," my mother smiled. "I'm just happy to have everyone here safe and sound."

We heard a commotion in the hallway. Ted instantly became rigid and at the ready.

"Is she in here!" A familiar voice shouted.

"Miss, you can't go in there," one of the nurses was telling her.

"The heck I can't!"

"Miss, I'm warning you."

"Thank you for your warning," Reba said, as she became visible in the doorway. "I'm sure I'll be fine!"

She came into the room, slightly out of breath, flipping her hair back behind her shoulders.

Rushing over to the bed, she said, "For crying out loud, Connie. Could you just make something easy for once?"

I smiled. There was nothing I could say to that. I felt the same way about myself most days.

"Not to make light of the situation, but if you'd have died, I'd be stuck working *you know where* for the rest of my life."

I laughed, and then stopped as a jolt of pain shot down my leg.

"That's new," I said. I looked up at Ted and asked, "Is that going to hurt forever?"

He shrugged. "Don't know, never been shot before."

"Well, you're a lot of help."

"I try," He winked.

"Well, listen," Reba interrupted. She pulled a small stuffed Teddy bear out from behind her back. "I'm going to give you this now because I don't know how much longer Nurse Ratched is going to let me stay in here."

"How sweet," I said, taking the bear and nuzzling my nose into it. It looked really soft. Unfortunately, it wasn't.

"It was the best I could do on short notice," Reba shrugged. "Next time, let me know when you're going to go get yourself shot, okay?"

"Will do," I gave a faint thumbs up.

My mother stared at me with annoyed eyes.

I swallowed hard. "Of course, this is hopefully going to be the last time anything like this ever happens again."

"Yeah right," Reba rolled her eyes. "Until next month."

"Boy, I hope not," I said.

"Me too," my mother agreed.

"Me three," Ted chuckled.

"Oh, brother," Reba sighed. "I'll see you when you get out of this place, okay," she said, resting her hand on my foot through the blankets. "Call me up when you're ready to get to work on that coffee shop you're always talking about." She winked and then tensed her body up and crouched down. "Now, all I have to do is get past that nasty woman without being seen and my mission will be complete."

At that moment, Nurse Ratched, who was actually called Nurse Bonnie, came into the room.

"What's that you say about getting past *that nasty woman*?"

For the first time ever I saw Reba blush and become speechless.

She made a weird face, with wide eyes and a half smile, before giving a very awkward wave and holding her hand in the shape of a phone to her ears and mouthing the words *call me* before she shimmied along the back wall of the room and out into the hallway.

"That one a friend of yours?" the nurse asked.

"Yup," I nodded.

"Takes all kinds, I guess," she smiled.

We all laughed.

25

It was about two weeks after my short but necessary visit to the hospital and I was back to work, planning out my true vision for *Connie's Cafe*.

I thought it fitting that the first order to arrive were the tables and chairs for the deck. I had a variety of them, all rod iron and with very elaborate designs.

Some of the tables had room for as many as eight people to sit and drink coffee and enjoy the view. Others were smaller, and more intimate, for couples who wanted to go out but be left alone in their own little bubbles of love.

Reba and Ted helped get them set up on the deck, while my mother checked over the invoices to make sure I wasn't *getting ripped off*.

I was on a pair of crutches, directing Ted and Reba as

they diligently set to work putting the ten tables and thirty-six chairs in place.

When they were finished, we ordered pizza and mom drove home to get a few bottles of chilled wine. She came back with bottles of Moscato, Pinot Grigio, and a Beaujolais for Ted, who refused to drink white wine with pizza.

"I think these will do the trick," she smiled as she came onto the deck. "Ted and Reba, could you run and get the glasses from my car? It's parked out front. And I think I saw the pizza delivery boy on his way too."

"Sure thing, Mrs. Cafe," Ted stood.

"Do I have to?" Reba sulked. "I'm so tired. I've been lugging this furniture around for hours."

"Actually," my mother looked at her watch. "It was less than forty-five minutes. And the delivery men brought everything up here for you."

"Good point," Reba said, standing up and joining Ted in fetching of the glasses and our food.

My mother sat down next to me at one of the big tables and we sat there for a minute, silently looking out over the creek.

"This is quite the place," my mother smiled. "I'm so proud of you."

I shook my head. "It never would've happened without you pushing me."

"That may be true," she nodded. "But sometimes, a person can be pushed and pushed and pushed, and never budge. You listened and prayed and, through the help of

God, and some rather unorthodox methods, it came to be."

"I just wish dad could see it," I smiled. "What do you think he would say?"

"I think he would tell you how much he loved you. He would tell you that he's beyond proud of you. And he would tell you that it's perfect." A small stream of tears gently rolled down her cheek. "Or, he would be so happy and his heart would be so full that he might not be able to say anything."

Those were the words I was hoping to hear. I took a deep cleansing breath in and felt the sun on my skin as a gentle breeze tousled my hair.

"I did it, dad," I whispered. "I did it."

THANK you so much for reading, Ligature & Latte. If you enjoyed the small town of Coffee Creek, then you'll want to check out the next books in the series! Check them out HERE!

READ THE FIRST TWO CHAPTERS
OF THE NEXT BOOK!

Thank you so much for reading Ligature & Latte!

To read the first two chapters of the next book in the series, Autumn & Autopsies, just keep going!

Thanks and God Bless,
Maisy

MAISY MARPLE

AUTUMN &
AUTOPSIES

Book Three in the Connie Cafe Mystery Series

AUTUMN & AUTOPSIES
CHAPTER ONE

I've always thought there was something magical about Autumn.

Apples and pumpkins.

Cool-weather and sweaters.

Warm Cider donuts and fresh pressed cider.

Homemade pies and thick, hearty stews.

Trips to the orchard and Fall Festivals.

I'm Connie Cafe, and ever since I was a little girl, I would embrace the cold Autumn air and brave the elements to sit with my father as he drank piping hot black coffee on the front porch of our old farmhouse on the outskirts of Coffee Creek.

We'd talked about all sorts of things before he passed away when I was in college. There are a lot of conversations I don't remember, but his love of coffee is impossible to forget.

After he died, I left college and came back home to live with my mother, Roberta Cafe. She has always pushed me to do amazing things with my life. Most recently, she encouraged me to open *Connie's Cafe* on Main Street in Coffee Creek. She and my best friend Reba were also instrumental (perhaps, a little too instrumental) in getting Officer Ted Billings and me together. I was fuming at first, but after a month, I can say life could have been much worse.

Things have been interesting since last May. I was a suspect in the murder of David Gardner, the best golfer in Coffee Creek, and most recently, my real estate agent, James Popper, was murdered on the deck of the building I'd purchased from him to start my cafe. Things were a little stressful, to say the least, and I had to lean on God a lot.

I was hopeful that as we geared up for Fall, things would slow down in the murder department so I could put my focus where it really belonged — getting *Connie's Cafe* off the ground.

Even though summer was over, and I missed a very busy season in our touristy little town, I was hopeful that turning the corner into Autumn would be a good experience. With all of the festivals and activities that were planned, I figured enough people would be out and about that we could drum up some good business heading into the winter.

My hope was that we could use the Fall season to gain experience and a little bit of money for when we really geared up in the mid to late spring for the summer tourist season the following year.

These thoughts were running through my head as I entered the kitchen in our old farmhouse. My mother was looking chic as ever in a bright yellow pantsuit, her flaming red hair styled to perfection.

She flashed me a grin as I walked in and held up my massive coffee mug. "I've got you covered. Just waiting on the gurgle now."

The gurgle was what she referred to as the sound the coffee maker makes just before it's all done making the coffee. I don't know where she picked it up. But to her credit, when I hear that sound now, it definitely does sound like a gurgle.

"Thanks," I said. "You know me too well."

"I should. I raised you, for heaven's sake."

I nodded. "That you did."

The gurgle happened, and my mother got her daily look of excitement as she turned and took the pot from the burner. She poured us each a tall, hot cup of steaming black coffee. Black as black could be.

"Thank you," I nodded, bringing the mug to my nose and doing the required ceremonial sniffing of the morning brew. "Perfection!"

"Agreed!" My mother took her first sip of the day and shook her head. "I don't think there's anything better in this world than that first sip of coffee in the morning."

"It's pretty tough to top," I agreed.

We moved to the table and sat down.

"So, what do you have going on today?" My mother asked.

"Reba and I are going to meet up at the shop and finish getting everything set up. We have some equipment that we need to finish moving around, and a few supply orders are due for delivery today, too. I want to be ready for this weekend and take advantage of the festival." Being the third week in September, the town of Coffee Creek had its annual *Apple Festival*. Aside from the summer months, this was by far the biggest money ticket for the town. It brought tourists in from hundreds of miles away to get the last perfect glimpse of Coffee Creek before winter came in and pretty much shut the town down. "It should bring quite a bit of extra foot traffic through town. I can't think of a better time to open the doors and give it a go."

"Do you need any help?"

I shrugged. "I'll let you know when the festival's over, I suppose. Honestly, I have no idea what to expect. I think we've got enough to get us through, and Reba's made coffee during the morning rush at the *place we do not name*. I don't think too much is going to frazzle either of us at this point."

"Well, let me know if I can be of service."

"Will do," I said, taking another large sip off my mug. "Thanks for everything, mom."

"Oh, it's nothing at all, dear." She put her hand on mine. "I'm sure this weekend will go swimmingly for you and Reba as you set off on yet another new adventure."

As I PARKED my car and stepped out onto the sidewalk outside *Connie's Cafe*, excitement washed over me. I'd dreamt about this for so many years, and it was finally here.

The custom sign that I'd ordered had been put up yesterday. While I'd seen the guys hang it, I hadn't gotten a good glimpse of it from the vantage of someone driving up to the cafe.

It did not disappoint. It was bright yellow with a fantastic pink scroll with the name *Connie's Cafe* positioned in the center —large and clear. In each corner of the sign was a single roasted coffee bean.

Simple.

That's the beauty of most things in this world. The simplest things have always been the ones that bring me the most joy. Trust in God, loving family and friends, wonders of nature, a good book, and a cup of coffee. It doesn't get much better than that.

I headed up the steps and into the shop, turning the

key before disabling the alarm. There was a sign in the doorway window with our hours of operation. It was a much better sign than what had been there a month earlier when Mable Wilson had paid a teenager named Piper to write awful messages about me being a murderer and posted them all over town.

That seemed like forever ago, a nightmare from the distant past, as I readied myself to open the doors in preparation for our first day of business.

I stood in the doorway and took a look around the inside dining area. Sturdy wooden tables and padded high-back chairs were arranged in a simple way. Five in all, each seating up to four people. I could have fit seven tables in the space, but it was important for me to have people feel comfortable while they were there. I didn't want my customers to feel like they had to sit on someone's lap to drink a cup of coffee and enjoy a conversation with a friend.

The display counter had been completely cleaned out from top to bottom. Reba, as I would have expected, made it very clear that she hated every minute of that. But to her credit, she helped me with it for the better part of four hours the day before.

It looked just marvelous, ready for the beautiful array of pastries and baked goods that I'd be making to serve up with our coffee, which would be second to none. I'd made sure of that, sourcing our beans from only the best local roasters around until I could figure things out enough to start roasting them myself in the back of the cafe.

The counter was clean and organized, with three coffee makers and two blenders. The sink was set up to rinse blenders and coffee pots quickly. We had a wide array of pump syrups and stacks of cups all ready to go.

It was exactly as I wanted it.

Reba came up the steps to the shop and stood in the doorway. She looked like death warmed over. Her purple hair was draped in front of her face, and she was hunched over and panting, like walking up the stairs had completely taken it out of her.

"Are you okay?" I asked.

She held a finger up, the universal sign that I needed to give her a minute to catch her breath before she could answer.

"I'll be fine, boss," she uttered through the strands of hair that were sticking to her mouth. "I'm here to work."

"Oh, no," I said. I walked around the counter and put my arm around her, guiding her to the closest chair. I sat down opposite her. "You need to go home and rest. I can take care of this."

"No, no, no," she shook her head. Droplets of water dripped all over the tabletop closest to us. *I'd have to wipe those up, so the table didn't end up with water stains,* I thought to myself.

"I told you I was gonna help," she said. Her voice sounded like she was on the verge of tears. "I can't let you down, or you're going to send me back to that awful place."

"That's not true," I smiled. "I would never send you back to that awful place. But I am going to send you home." I stood up and took her by the hand, leading her back toward the door. "You take the day and rest, and I'll get things situated around here."

Reba stopped on the third step down and looked back up at me. "Are you sure?"

"Absolutely," I nodded. "I've got this."

"Thanks," she said, and then she got into her car to drive home.

I smiled and waved as she pulled out from her spot. As soon as she was out of view, I went back inside, closed the door, and screamed at the top of my lungs.

AUTUMN & AUTOPSIES
CHAPTER TWO

"Mom," I barked into my phone. "I need your help."

I explained to my mother what had happened with Reba. I felt bad asking her to come in and bail me out yet again. But there was no way I was going to be able to get everything done on my own.

In typical Roberta Cafe fashion, she did not disappoint. She was at the shop in less than twenty minutes, still dressed to perfection in her bright yellow pantsuit and ready to work.

It always amazed me how she could work so hard and get so much done and yet, never look like she'd even broken a sweat. She looked every bit as good when we were finished as she had when we had begun.

"Is there anything else?" She asked. It was getting on

to late afternoon, and we had worked our tails off, getting everything perfect for the next day. Everything had been wiped and polished within an inch of its life. All of the prep work for the baked goods had been done as much as it could be, and the coffee was set and ready to percolate.

"No," I shook my head, standing behind the register, looking around at what my invitation to Coffee Creek was going to be. "I think we outdid ourselves today. Thanks, mom."

"It was my pleasure," she said, putting her arm around my shoulders. I instinctively laid my head down on hers. "You know, if Reba can't make it in tomorrow, I'm not a bad little coffee slinger myself."

"I know, mom," I chuckled. "I know you're very good at pouring black coffee."

"What?" My mother feigned offense. "All I'm saying is that if you get in a jam tomorrow and Reba can't be here, call me up and I'll come in and pour black coffee all day long. Plus, I saw that coffee cake you've got on the menu. I would take a piece of that as payment, you know?"

"We'll see," I smiled. "Hey, we have a few hours until dinner—"

"Which is going to be pizza…delivered to the house. I don't care how much the delivery charge is."

"Sounds good to me. I was thinking we could head over to McDougall's Orchard and pick some apples, maybe enjoy a nice warm cider donut and a cup of mulled cider. Plus, I'd like to find some nice gourds for the tables. What do ya say?"

"That sounds lovely," my mother smiled.

McDougall's orchard was already bursting at the seams with people eager to get started with the big weekend. They had two buildings. One was a massive green pole barn that they used to sell pre-picked fruit. They also handed out bags for U-pick.

The other building was about a quarter-mile walk on the same side of the road. It was red and much smaller. This building had pre-picked fruit as well, but most people stopped by this shop for the local fruit wines, specialty meats and cheeses, freshly baked pies, and homemade fudge…plus warm cider donuts and fresh pressed apple cider.

Behind both of these buildings, there were places to pick apples, strawberries, blueberries, grapes, cherries, and peaches. On the opposite side of the road, they had apple trees as far as the eye could see. There was also a small playground for the kids and a tractor for hayrides. And, of course, they had a small but tricky corn maze.

My mother and I parked our cars at the pole barn first.

"Hey, mom," I said as we were walking up to look at

their selection of gourds. "What do ya say we check out the corn maze before we leave?"

"I don't know," she crinkled her face. "I've never liked those things. I always get the feeling that something bad's going to happen when I'm in there."

"Like what?" I laughed. "It's a family-owned orchard, not some Stephen King novel out in Nebraska, for crying out loud."

"I know that," she slapped my arm. "I just get the heebie-jeebies when I'm stuck in something like that."

I shrugged. "Alright, suit yourself. You can head home and order the pizza, and I'll do the corn maze by myself."

"You know," she raised an eyebrow in my direction, "every now, and then I look at you, and I'm so impressed with the grown-up, mature, thoughtful woman you've become."

"Aww, mom, that's so sweet." I hugged her.

"Now is not one of those times."

I let go of her and stood back my mouth agape. "Why, I never…"

She winked at me, and we went inside to see what we could find.

Amanda Yerdon was at the helm. She was standing next to the register, pointing out where things were for people.

Amanda was a heavy-set woman in her mid-fifties. She'd worked at the orchard for as long as I could remember.

"Hey, Roberta!" She called out. "Hey, Connie!"

"Hey, Amanda!" We called back.

"How's business this year?" My mother asked as she walked over to the register.

Amanda held out her arms. "It's pretty busy. That ain't a bad thing." She gave a faint smile that told me she might have just been saying that so as not to offend anybody. Her frazzled hair and red, sweat-speckled face told a different story.

The pole barn was filled with people. A few families, several others on their own, and of course, there were some mother-daughter pairs. I didn't recognize most of the people, which was a good sign for this coming weekend.

"No, it's not," my mother shook her head. "The festival hasn't even really started yet, and you're this busy. Imagine what tomorrow and Saturday are going to bring."

"Tell me about it," Amanda nodded. "And this ain't even the half of it. Go back outside and take a look up the hill. The lines up there have been insane today. Insane, I tell ya!"

My mother and I walked back out of the barn and out into the parking lot and looked up at the red building. Sure enough, that parking lot was so full that people had started to park on the side of the road. And the line of people was even more *insane* than Amanda had led us to believe."

"Is this typical?" My mother asked Amanda as we went back inside.

She shook her head, wiping sweat from her brow with a folded-up bandana she had taken from the back pocket of her jeans.

"No, it's not typical. This is the first year we tried out that social media thing. I'm not that up on it, but Mr. McDougall hired someone to run some of those…I forgot what he called them." She snapped her fingers and gave her head a few open-palmed slaps. "*Think, Amanda, think….*"

"It's okay." My mother tried to comfort her. "I don't know that much about—"

"Campaigns!" Amanda blurted out.

"Oh, yeah," my mother nodded, pretending she knew what Amanda was talking about.

I'd be lying if I said that I didn't find it mildly amusing to watch my mother and Amanda talk about the world of social media, something of which, it was obvious, they knew nothing about.

"Yeah," Amanda nodded. "So we fired up our socials, and boom! The people just showed up. It's been crazy, I tell ya. Just crazy. Heck, we might have to hire three more people before tomorrow just to keep up with everything. I'm joking, of course, but you get the idea."

I was quite impressed by the sheer volume of people that were at McDougall's on a Thursday evening in the third week of September.

I was also quite bummed about it, as it meant that my dreams of hot, fluffy donuts and spicy warm cider were going by the wayside.

"Congratulations on your huge spike in traffic," I nodded at Amanda.

"Yeah, thanks," she said, blowing a curly lock of dyed brown hair out of her face. "I just hope I can keep up with it," she laughed.

We left the pole barn with nothing to show for it. Well, almost nothing to show for it.

My mother now thought she was a social media expert.

"You should get up on those *socials*," she suggested as we walked out toward our cars.

"Oh, you think so?" I stifled a laugh.

"What?!?" My mother said, clearly aware that I was doing everything I could not make fun of her.

"Nothing," I said. "What do you say we take a walk across the street and just stroll through the orchard for a little while."

"I'm getting pretty tired," she said.

"I understand," I nodded. "Do you want to head home and get the pizza ordered? I'll be home in a little while."

She agreed, and I headed across the street to one of my favorite places in the whole world.

Walking through row after row of apple trees, the

smell of every kind of apple one could imagine hung in the air.

I always felt so at one with God when I was walking through the orchard. The idea is that you could plant something like a tree, and in just a few years, with some careful tending, it would produce the most amazing fruits — the sustenance of all life. It was just awesome. And when I say *awesome*, I don't mean something that's really neat. I mean something that is literally awe-inspiring, something that is sent down from on high for us to enjoy to the fullest.

I'd walked through a few rows when I saw something that sent a shock through my heart.

Ted was walking through the orchard rows as well. He had on a pair of dress shorts and a red polo. I wasn't anywhere near him, but I could smell his mint gum and cologne just the same. It had become something of a pavlovian response whenever he was around.

Unfortunately, he had another woman walking with him. And she was close. Closer than close. They weren't holding hands or anything like that, but they certainly bumped elbows a few times.

"Hey, Connie!" Ted waved when we were about a hundred feet from each other. "I didn't expect to see you here."

I bet you didn't, I thought.

Thankfully, what I said was, "Yeah, I came over with my mother, but she got tired and had to go home. I just couldn't pull myself away without a walk through the trees, ya know."

"Absolutely," he nodded. "Hey, I want you to meet someone," he said, bringing his eyes over to the girl on his arm. She was gorgeous and easily five years younger than me. She wore form-fitting jeans, bright white tennis shoes, and a less-than-modest black and white polka dot blouse. Her sandy blond hair was flowing in the breeze as she seductively sipped on a styrofoam cup of steaming mulled cider.

"Oh yeah," I nodded, trying hard to hide my hurt.

"Yeah," he nodded. "Connie, this is my cousin Lacey Bennett. Lacey just got in from New York today."

"Oh, wow," I laughed. I could feel myself blushing and starting to breathe heavily as I let out one deep sigh after another. "I thought you were...Um...I just didn't expect...."

"I know, right!" Ted laughed. "She didn't tell me she was coming. It was a total surprise for me too!"

"Fantastic."

"Nice to meet you," Lacey smiled, reaching her hand out.

"Sorry," Ted said, realizing he hadn't told Lacey who I was yet. "This is Connie. She's my...."

"Girlfriend," I filled in the word for him.

"Yes," he smiled. "Connie's my girlfriend."

We shook hands and then stood there awkwardly for a few moments before I said, "Well, I'm just going to finish up my walk and then head home. Roberta, believe it or not, is going to order pizza for dinner *on a weeknight.*"

"Wow," Ted's eyes lit up. "She must be really tired. Did you work her to the bone today?"

"Something like that," I winked. "Anyway, I'm sure I'll see you around, Lacey. Listen, if you get some time tomorrow, why don't you come down to Main Street and have a cup of coffee on me."

"Sounds great!" She chirped.

"I'll give you a call later," Ted said as he and Lacey continued on their walk.

"Sounds like a plan," I smiled.

It had been a crazy day.

What else could possibly happen?

Tap Here to Keep Reading

BECOME A VIP READER!

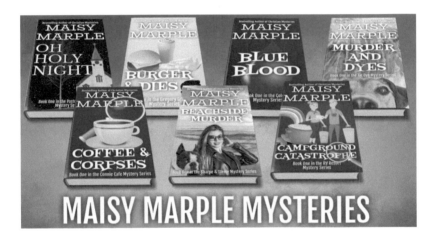

To get updates on current projects and gain access to special contests and prizes, click on the image and sign up!

ALSO BY MAISY MARPLE

Visit Maisy Marple's Author Page on Amazon to read any of the titles below!

Connie Cafe Series

Coffee & Corpses

Ligature & Latte

Autumn & Autopsies

Pumpkins & Poison

Death & Decaf

Turkey & Treachery

Mistletoe & Memories

Snow & Sneakery

Repairs & Renovations

Bagels & Bible Study

S'more Jesus

Proverbs & Preparations

Sharpe & Steele Series

Beachside Murder

Sand Dune Slaying

Boardwalk Body Parts

RV Resort Mystery Series

Campground Catastrophe

Bad News Barbecues

Sunsets and Bad Bets

Short Stories

Forty Years Together

Long Story Short

The Best Gift of All

Miracle at the Mall

The Ornament

The Christmas Cabin

Cold Milk at Midnight

Short Story Collections

Hot Cocoa Christmas

Unapologetically Christian Essays

Reason for the Season

God is Not Santa Claus

Free Will is Messy

Fear Not

Not About this World

We Are All Broken

Veritas

God Ain't Your Butler

An Argument for Hate

Agape Love (With Pastor Michael Golden)

Addiction Help

Hard Truths: Overcoming Alcoholism One Second At A Time

ABOUT THE AUTHOR

Maisy Marple is a lover of small town cozy mysteries, plus she has a wicked coffee habit to boot. She loves nothing more than diving into a clean mystery with a cup of the darkest, blackest coffee around.

She grew up in a small town and now lives in the country, giving her more than enough inspiration for creating the cozy locales and memorable characters that are on display in her Connie Cafe Mystery Series!

Also, she hates social media — so you won't find her there.

To connect with Maisy, sign up for her VIP reader list and get a free mystery story. Check out the offer on the previous page.

Made in United States
Troutdale, OR
12/11/2024